Run or Dye

Aurora Aspen Magical Holiday Mysteries, Volume 3

Paula Lester

Published by Paula Lester, 2021.

Copyright Notice

This is a work of fiction. Similarities to real people, places, or events are entirely coincidental.
Run or Dye
First edition. May 30, 2021.
Copyright © 2021 Paula Lester
Written by Paula Lester
Cover Design by Jane Hinchey
Proofreading by Liz Borino

Chapter 1

I gasped for breath, shoving a fist into my side in a lame attempt to get rid of the cramp.

Cam, my handsome and long-suffering boyfriend, had no empathy for the fact that I wasn't getting enough air into my lungs. "Are you done?"

"I think so. Hold on." I straightened and tipped my head to look him over again. Then, I erupted into another round of belly-laughter, doubling over as my abdomen spasmed again.

"Apparently not," Cam said with an eye-roll. "What, exactly, is so funny about this?"

Gulping in air again and trying to get control of myself, I squeaked, "I don't know. Nothing. Everything." I squinted at him. "You look so funny."

He glanced down and took in the splotches of color all over his shirt, shorts, legs, and sneakers. "Did you think I was going to come out of it neat and tidy, Rory? It was a color run. I thought being all colorfully dyed at the end was pretty much the point."

"It was. You look...great." I pressed my lips together and tried to be serious. It was hard because his face was covered with purple, pink, green, and blue pastel splotches. His hair stood up in colorful spikes where he must have run a hand through it while it was wet with dye. "You're always so put to-gether. It's weird to see you messy."

He raised a particularly purple eyebrow. "Nice try. Not buying it."

I smirked.

"You look like you tried to paint a baby's nursery and the paint won."

Cam and I turned to watch my friend Isla approach. She was also colorfully dyed with pastels, but somehow, it made her look even more fashionable than usual rather than comical.

"Okay, okay, I get it. I don't look good in the spring color palette. I'll make sure to keep that in mind next time I go make-up shopping." Cam chuckled good-naturedly. "You, on the oth-er hand, look fantastic with that pink hair. How about a hug? We can make our clothes match." He winked.

I held up my hands and backed away. "Nope. I didn't run the 5K, so I don't deserve to have such lovely colors all over my clothes. I'll live vicariously through both of you and settle for pink only in my hair."

White shorts, shirt, and sneakers probably hadn't been the best choice for hosting a color run. I'd spent most of the morn-ing trying to stay on the right side of the breeze, so dye didn't end up all over me. Maybe I could distract Cam from locking me in a messy bear hug with a change of subject. "You both had fast times. How many people are still out on the trails?" I turned to Mira, the employee who had quickly risen to become my right-hand woman.

She consulted a laptop on the plastic foldable table in front of her. "Looks like twenty are in and we have another twelve or so out."

I shook my head in amazement. "That's so cool. I never would have thought to order number bibs with traceable chips in them."

Mira waved a hand. "It was Roger's idea. He turned me on to this company and helped me download the right app, so we could monitor the runners and walkers."

"It was a *great* idea. This way, I don't have to worry about anyone getting lost or hurt and being stranded on a trail with no one knowing where they are." Shady Corners had over a hundred miles of trails in and immediately surrounding the city limits. They were heavily used for walking, trail-running, mountain biking, and cross-country skiing. Though they were fairly well-marked, it was possible to get turned around if you missed a sign or two.

My business, Aspen Events, didn't need any bad publicity like a lost or hurt event participant. It had already been on the periphery of a couple not-so-great occurrences recently.

To be specific, two events had ended with murder victims. I was trying to garner goodwill with the community and prove it was safe to have us plan and manage events.

"The chips and the app were a good idea," Cam confirmed. "But so was hosting this event to raise money for the animal shelter in the first place." He gave me a sidelong look. "I'm sure you're losing money on the deal."

"I'm happy to put on a fundraiser that can help with name recognition for Aspen Events. Plus, you know I love me some shelter pets."

A loud thwomp drew our attention to the race's finish line, where a runner had come through and been shot with purple dye by the attendant there.

The dye-blasting guns set up at intervals along the course were louder than I'd anticipated, and they kept making me jump. I was on edge because this event needed to go off without a hitch. My business may hinge on it.

I smiled as all the spectators lined up along the finish line cheered and hooted at the splotchy finisher. At least the Run or Dye 5K was well-attended, and everyone seemed to be having fun.

"I'm thinking about adopting a chinchilla from the animal shelter." Isla grabbed an apple from the snack table laid out for athletes and crunched it.

I raised both eyebrows, my friend's announcement completely distracting me from my previous musings. "What would Ivan think about that?"

"He's indifferent."

I highly doubted Isla's cat wouldn't have strong feelings about a pet rodent suddenly hanging out in his space, taking some of his owner's attention, but I knew better than to argue with my best friend. She was the only person I'd ever met who was more stubborn than me.

Besides, I'd love to have a soft, cuddly chinchilla to snuggle with when I visited Isla.

Instead of engaging, I turned back to Mira, twisting around to perch on the plastic table to face her. I had to compete with the computer screen for her attention and lost. She didn't even glance at me. "So, things are going well with you and Roger?" I winced at myself. Why did I use that annoying sing-songy tone when asking about Mira's romantic life? Because it was a time-honored tradition? Someone should kill that tradition—it was awful. But it was too late. I'd already done it and couldn't take it back. May as well add me to the ranks of super annoying people digging for info about a single person's dating status, such as every woman's great-aunt at every family event ever.

Mira spared me a glance and a wrinkled nose, as if my tone of voice actually came with a rotten smell. I clamped my lips shut, hoping she didn't get a whiff of coffee breath or something. "Okay, I guess."

"Only okay?" Isla asked from behind me, speaking around the bite of apple still in her mouth.

Mira's cheeks colored. She didn't answer right away. Finally, she grinned and glanced up at us. "I think it's going great. But I keep waiting for the other shoe to drop. I don't want to jinx it."

"What shoe? Why would it drop?" I demanded.

She looked away again. "I don't know—the shoe that always drops in my life. Roger's so handsome and doing so well. I keep wondering what he would see in me."

I opened my mouth to argue, but Isla elbowed me, and when I jerked around to see why, she jutted out her chin. My gaze followed her gesture. Roger, the object of Mira's shoe-dropping angst, was approaching. I snapped my mouth shut and gave him a smile.

Probably looked fake, but it was the best I could do on short notice.

"I got the snack sticks!" Roger put a plastic tub of jerky on the table. Then he made a beeline for Mira and swept her up in a hug.

Yeah, Mira doesn't have anything to worry about. This guy is smitten.

Mira hugged him back, a bright smile on her face. "Having a chef for a boyfriend comes in handy, especially when you're trying to find protein-rich snacks for athletes."

"Hey, I provided protein!" Isla protested. "Look at all that cheese. Nuts too!"

I patted her shoulder, careful to avoid the smudge of yellow dye near her neck. "You're a great chef. It's not a competition."

She stuck out her tongue at me and tossed the apple core in a trash bag.

"Rory, there you are!"

I turned in the direction of my mother's voice. She held Piper's leash and walked next to my dad. I waved, glad to see them. Piper wiggled so hard it looked like she might squiggle right out of her skin, so I dropped to one knee to give the sweet German shorthaired pointer a hug and some kisses.

I caught a glimpse of white fur, but by the time I turned in that direction, it was gone. There was very little doubt in my mind that I'd seen Sasha, my mom's and my cat familiar. She was always around lately, very seldom more than a hundred feet or so away from me. She took her job protecting me from the evil wizard, Xavier, seriously.

Much to my everlasting chagrin.

"This is so nice, honey." Mom looked through Jackie O-style round, gold-rimmed sunglasses at the field dotted with spectators, finished racers, and even reporters with cameras. "It's a good thing we had nice weather for it today."

"I know—it was a roll of the dice." Early April in Shady Corners could produce any kind of weather, from seventy degrees and sunny to blizzard conditions or a torrential rainstorm.

Dad said, "It was nice of you to do this for Candace. She's got her hands full over at the animal rescue, that's for sure. The money from this event may be what allows her to stay open for a while longer."

Mira, an arm still around Roger's waist, piped up, "That's true. You know, Candace is one of my closest friends. She's put nearly every dime of her own money into that shelter, but the landlord keeps raising the rent. She can't find an appropriate place to move that would be as nice for housing all the shelter animals. It's been a real worry for her lately, and this event is going to take a load off her mind, at least for a little while."

Roger squeezed Mira. "Candace is a good egg. She does so much for the stray animals of Shady Corners. It's nice to see the community giving back to her. I wish that stingy landlord of hers would lighten up on her. But, then again, I wish he'd lighten up on me too." He snorted. "He holds the lease to my catering business also."

"Who's her landlord again?" I tipped my head, trying to sift through the list of our town's building owners in my mind.

"Strom Pearson." Roger said the name with a slight wrinkle of his nose. "The man, the myth, the miser."

"Ah. I've heard of him." Not for the first time, I was glad I owned the office building where my event planning business was housed. Actually, technically, the bank owned it, but I paid the mortgage. Okay, even more technically, Dad paid the mortgage some months, but my business was doing better, and that wouldn't be the case for very much longer. Assuming, of course, I could convince everyone in Shady Corners it was safe to use Aspen Events because it was a total coincidence there had been two murders at my parties.

Total, *complete* coincidence.

"Strom is actually a runner in this event," Mira said. "Not sure why he would show his face here, but I guess he's just that smug."

Shouts rang out from across the field, drawing all our attention. "What's going on?" I wondered out loud, holding a hand over my eyes and squinting to see better. People moved fast, like ants over dropped fruit, toward the spot where the shouting had occurred, which was the 5K's finish line.

"An athlete's down!" Cam was moving toward the commotion before the words were out of his mouth, Roger hot on his heels.

The rest of us dashed after the men, my parents moving the slowest behind the rest of us. Since I hated running—because...is it good for your joints? I've always gone with no, it's not. Who wants to ruin their joints? Or have to buy sneakers every three months? Not this girl. I'll just keep walking slowly, thank you very much—I arrived a good thirty seconds after Cam and Roger. I pushed my way through the crowd, even throwing a few elbows, to arrive next my boyfriend.

"What's going on?" I repeated, but as I emerged into an open space, I could see for myself. A runner lay unmoving on the ground. I knew red wasn't one of the dye colors we'd used along the course. So, it was obvious the streaks of red interspersed with the various pastels all over the guy's clothes and skin wasn't dye. It was blood.

Cam knelt next to the man and reached for his neck. One side sported a huge open wound, blood trickling where it had spurted moments before. Cam switched to touch the other side. "I don't feel a pulse." He gave me a shocked look over his shoulder. "Someone call 9-1-1. I think he's dead."

I'm embarrassed to say my first thought was, *Oh, no. Not again.*

Chapter 2

"Get away from my husband!" A woman shoved me away from the fallen runner and threw herself over him. Her sobs jerked both their bodies around.

Dimly, I heard Cam directing people away from the area, but it was as though I'd grown roots to the spot. How could this be happening again?

As an ambulance careened onto the lawn, sirens blaring, a man and woman stepped up to the grieving woman. The man spoke into her ear, and they gently helped her to her feet and moved her aside, so the EMTs could get to her.

The medical team checked the man out for a few minutes, then one shook his head at the other.

The runner's wife wailed louder at that. A police cruiser arrived, followed by two more. Within minutes, the runner was loaded into the ambulance, which left silently, sirens and lights off.

Officers led the man's wife to the finish line, where she collapsed onto a chair.

"This 5K was supposed to convince people my events are safe to book and attend." Disbelief coursed through me. "I swear, Aspen Events is cursed."

Isla threw an arm around my shoulders and squeezed. "It's not cursed. It's unlucky. Perhaps slightly hexed. But not cursed. At least, I don't think so. Are curses real? You'd know better than me."

"Curses are very real." Sasha's voice came from near our feet. "I don't sense one around Aurora, though. She has extraordinarily bad luck, that's all. Bad taste in sneakers too."

"Stuff it, cat," I snapped. "Not everybody can afford fancy, brand-name tennis shoes."

"No, but you could at least choose knockoffs that are more attractive. These make you look like you're straight out of the eighties. The nineteen-eighties, I mean. That decade had considerably worse fashion than the eighteen-eighties."

"The eighties were amazing," Isla said with a sigh. "I wish I'd been old enough to enjoy them more. We should bring them back."

"Your hair wouldn't survive the eighties," I scoffed.

"That's true. I never could grow any decent bangs." Isla's tone was mournful.

"Can we stay on topic here please?"

Sasha blinked a couple of times. "The topic at hand being that there was another murder at one of your events? And it's not because of a curse but merely bad luck?"

"We're sure it was a murder, then?" Isla released my shoulders and reached into her pocket. She pulled out a pack of gum and offered me a piece, which I refused. I hated chewing gum—it seemed like a lot of work for not much reward. I'd much rather use my daily chewing allotment for real food. Like donuts and muffins.

"The man had four or five holes punched into his neck and chest, from which he bled out almost immediately." Sasha's tone was wry. "I don't think he did that to himself, and I don't suppose someone *accidentally* nailed him with a shotgun."

I eyed the familiar. "Shotgun? You think it was a shotgun? Wouldn't somebody have heard that?"

Sasha did a cat version of a shrug, and I wondered, not for the first time, how she managed to pull that off with her feline body. "There was lots of noise around here. Those horrible color-guns made a huge racket."

She was right. The things had made me jumpy all morning. But the conversation with my friends and family had distracted me from them—had one gone off before the runner collapsed? I didn't know.

"Incoming," Isla muttered, giving Sasha a clue it was time to clam up.

"Rory!" Mira approached, wringing her hands. The fine lines around her eyes were deeper than usual. "Do you know who that was? The victim, I mean?"

I shook my head.

"Strom Pearson."

My jaw dropped. "The landlord we were talking about a few minutes ago?" What were the odds?

Mira wrung her hands. "I don't even understand why he was running here to begin with, but he was, and now he's...dead." She squeaked out the last word rather than speaking it.

"How is that possible? And what happened?" I glanced toward the finish line where cops swarmed the area. Actually, Shady Corners didn't have enough police officers to swarm anything. There were a few cops taking pictures, putting things in plastic bags, and otherwise securing the crime scene. Casey Norton, Shady Corners' acting sheriff, scribbled on a notepad as she spoke to Candace, the rescue shelter's director. Behind the women, a gloved officer put the dye-shooting gun into a clear plastic bag and marked it.

"From what I could gather before they shooed me away, something came out of the dye gun that wasn't dye, and it hit and killed Strom," Mira explained.

"That's crazy! Could it be that the gun is defective?" I wondered.

Mira shrugged. "I have no idea, but what a horrible way to go."

My parents and Piper approached. Dad shook his head. "Hard to believe Pearson's gone," he said. "And we were just talking about him." He echoed what I had been thinking earlier. "I didn't like the guy, myself, but this is unbelievable. Not to mention, it's the third murder in Shady Corners in a few months' time."

I winced. "And the third murder at one of my events. This is going to sink my business."

"I'm sure it will be fine, dear," Mom said. "No one could blame you for these things happening. It isn't your business's fault that killers keep choosing your events to strike."

I dropped my head back to look at the sky and groaned. Then I picked it back up and tipped it at Dad. "Why didn't you like Strom Pearson?"

"He's caused trouble in Shady Corners for a long time," Dad said. "Has a history of raising the rent on people to the point where they can't pay, and they lose their businesses. The city council has been trying to figure out how to edge him out of here for years, but he manages to operate far enough within the lines of the law to avoid too much blowback."

"Somebody may have decided to stop waiting for legal action to do the trick," Isla suggested.

"You mean you think someone may have killed Strom because of his practices as a landlord?" It made sense. Especially if what Dad and Mira had told me about Pearson so far was true.

Isla said, "It's an idea."

"It's a good idea," Dad confirmed. "Pearson was not well-liked, that's for sure."

Mom frowned. "Ms. Norton said we couldn't leave until she'd had a chance to question us." She glanced at Sasha, and I knew what she was thinking—that I'd be missing a day of training if this took too long.

The two of them—Mom and Sasha—were training me to use magic better. I'd known I was a witch from the time I was pretty young, but I hadn't realized the true extent of my capabilities until a few months earlier. For most of my life, I'd only enhanced holiday spirit with my power. I could boost patriotic feelings easily around Independence Day or nudge along romantic connections at Valentine's Day, for example.

But it turned out I was actually a spirit witch, which is crazy because it's something no one has seen before and most people in the world of magic didn't think existed.

As a spirit witch, I could draw from all the webs of energy that were always around. Holiday energy was always strongest, which was why it was easy for me to connect with that without training. But after a couple months of working with Mom and

Sasha, I knew how to tap into all the various energy lines, add my intention, and create the results I wanted.

And it was a good thing, too, because the two of them insisted an evil wizard named Xavier—my mother's boyfriend from high school, weirdly enough—was trying to find me, kill me, and take my spirit magic for himself.

They say exes can be bitter, but I felt like this was taking it way too far.

"Rory!"

I spun around to find Casey Norton approaching.

I steeled myself for the coming conversation and decided to head it off. I held up my hands. "Don't worry. I'll stay out of it. I'm not going to get involved in this investigation at all."

She stopped and regarded me from a few feet away, frowning. Then her eyes flitted to the others around me. "Can I talk to you alone for a minute, Aspen?"

My eyebrows slid upward like they rode an elevator. "Sure." I twisted to give my friends and family a bewildered look behind Norton's back as I followed her to a sidewalk at the edge of the green space. "What can I do for you?" I asked when she turned back around to face me.

"I want your help on this case."

"I swear I'm not going to get involved this time. You don't need to worry about it. I mean, I know I said that last time and everything but this time I actually mean it."

Norton thinned her lips. "Aspen. Focus. I said I *do* want your help."

Giving her the side eye, I bunched my forehead the way my mom always told me not to. *You're going to get permanent lines in the middle of your forehead, honey.* "Come again?"

Norton let out a longsuffering sigh, like someone who'd dealt with a horribly difficult person for far too long and was on the verge of giving up. From between gritted teeth, she hissed, "I. Want. Your. Help. On. This. Case. Please don't make me say it a fourth time. It's possible my head may explode."

I blinked through the shock fogging my brain. "I don't want that, that's for sure. But I'm confused. You've spent so much time lately telling me to mind my own business that this feels like...well, like you're setting me up like Lucy does Charlie Brown. Either that or you're suffering from a medical event or something that's completely changed your personality. Are you okay?"

"I'm fine," she snapped. "Except that I inherited this job before I was ready for it, and I don't have anyone working for me who can follow an investigative trail to save their lives. I swear, I'd be better off firing half the police department—which would only be half a dozen people, by the way—and hiring some reporters or something. At least they're trained investigators." She drew a breath, pulling up her shoulders and closing her eyes. She pinched the bridge of her nose as though she were working on a calming deep breathing exercise.

"Okay," I said slowly, drawing out the word. She wasn't doing that great at convincing me she wasn't having some kind of episode. I waited, not wanting to interrupt her breathing exercise and risk a full-blow eruption. Or an arrest. But a thought occurred to me, and I leaned forward to whisper, "I'm not a reporter either."

"I know!" she shouted, eyes popping open. She looked around, but no one was paying attention to us. Softer, she said, "I know you're not a reporter or a cop. But you're ridiculously nosy. And that seems to help with murder investigations. So, I want you to go ahead and do your nosy thing, with my blessing." She held up a finger to interrupt as I opened my mouth.

I snapped it shut again.

"You are not to do anything risky. I'm not giving you a gun or anything. But I will make you a deputy. And you'll get paid for your time."

My mouth sprang open again.

Norton held up a hand and tipped her head. "No. It won't be *good* pay. But it's better than nothing, since I know you'll be doing your nosy thing anyway, much as you swear you won't."

I resented that. How dare she suggest my promise not to get involved was a lie? Okay, it was a lie. I was already intrigued by Strom's murder and pretty much couldn't wait to figure out who'd killed him.

Out of the corner of my eye, I saw Candace still being questioned by an officer and felt the urge to go talk to her myself.

"If you need my help that much," I crossed my arms and cocked a hip, striking a self-important pose, "I guess it wouldn't be right to turn you down."

With a glare that could have made a rambunctious kindergartener straighten up and fly right, she reached into her breast pocket and pulled out a card, which she handed to me. "Here's your badge. It doesn't allow you to do anything other than ask people questions and get into the back door of the police department, so you can come directly to my office. Only when I call you and ask you to, though. No other time."

I peered at the picture of myself which stared back from the ID card. "Where did you get this? Why do you have it?" The photo could have been a mugshot. I wasn't looking at the camera, my face was screwed up in a strange position with one eye half-closed, and a chunk of hair stood straight out from the back of my head.

"It's a snapshot from the surveillance cameras in the conference room at the police department." She hooked her thumbs in her belt and settled back on her heels.

"Are you kidding me? This is terrible. Can't I come in and get a real picture taken?" I waved the card around. "My hair isn't even this color anymore."

She pursed her lips. "I liked the blue better. This pink is a little...jarring. Now that you work for the police department, you should probably stick to natural colors, though. That's what the HR department says."

"The HR department is only Roberta Hencock, and she doesn't follow up on that kind of thing, I know that for a fact. And I'm not dying my hair to a *natural color*. Certainly not for a job where I only get to talk, get no benefits and crappy pay, and can't even arrest people. It's basically what I already do."

"You absolutely cannot arrest people," she confirmed. "Fine. Keep your hair pink. Make an appointment with the forensics team for a better photo if you want, but do it on your own time. The department isn't paying for that."

I put the card an inch from my face, but it looked so much worse I pulled it back in disgust. "You can't even tell this is me. Let me see your picture. It's gotta be loads better than this."

"I'm not showing you my picture. Now, where are you planning on starting with the investigation?"

"Really? I didn't even accept the job, and you're being all bossy?"

She gave me a wry look.

"Fine. I accept the job. And I don't know. I was thinking about talking to Candace."

Casey adjusted her badge. "Since she shot the dye gun that killed Strom Pearson, I'd say that's a no-brainer." She spun on her heel. Over her shoulder, she said, "This is pretty much an open and shut case. I only need enough evidence for a prosecutor to present at court."

"Wait. I have no idea how to collect evidence properly for a prosecution." My tone was a twinge more panicky than I liked, and I cleared my throat to cover for it.

She stopped short and turned back, giving me a thoughtful look. "You're right. Better stop by the department and get a manual."

"A manual?" I parroted, feeling more befuddled by the second. It was like I'd walked into a funhouse room where up was down and Casey Norton had gone from steady and reliable to slightly mad. I expected the Cheshire cat to pop up on her shoulder any second. "There's a manual for how to be a cop? I thought you had to go to school."

She rolled her eyes. "It's specifically for deputized people—to go over the basics of what you can and can't say during an investigation. Go to the front desk and have the officer get one from Roberta for you."

"I should think about this more."

"Think fast. For all we know, the killer may strike again." She took off again, this time not slowing on her way to the patrol car.

I watched her back and contemplated what to do. Across the lawn, an officer slapped handcuffs on Candace and led her away, Mira chasing along.

A dozen or so dyed runners stood around gawking at the cops. The rest of the racers must have left after Strom collapsed. So much for the winner's ceremony we'd been planning.

As I trudged over to help Cam and Jed, who were working on packing things into the Aspen Events van, I thought about Candace and wondered if they'd gotten the right person. Casey must have some doubts about that, to hire me to investigate and warn me about the killer striking again.

Was she right? Or did the animal rescue group director finally get fed up and take the shot at getting rid of her landlord?

Chapter 3

It took a while for the cops to finish their evaluation of the crime scene. My parents left with Piper after Mom said she'd wait at home for me to do some training. Sasha had disappeared too, but you never knew with her. She always seemed to be nearby, ready to appear at a moment's notice to explain how I was doing things all wrong.

By the time the cops had left, all our stuff was loaded into my truck, Jed had left to return it to my office, and Isla and I had cleaned up all the random trash and remaining race stuff from the lawn, I was still wondering if I'd made the right decision accepting Casey's offer. I was finishing up explaining it all to Isla when Mira pulled up and jumped out of her car.

She hurried over to us. "They're booking Candace for the murder. She has a court date in an hour or so, and I'm on-call to pick her up if she posts bail." There were new bags under Mira's eyes, like she'd been awake for two days since the last time I saw her an hour ago. "She didn't do this. I know she didn't."

Isla asked, "Did she say if she had any suspicions about who did?"

Mira shook her head. "We didn't have time to talk. In fact, I only saw her for a couple minutes in the police department lobby. Only enough time for her to ask me to pick her up if she posts bail and tell me she didn't do it. But she didn't have to tell me that—I already knew it. Candace is one of my best friends, and she absolutely doesn't have it in her to hurt someone. I mean, look at what she does all day every day for the shelter animals." Tears jumped into Mira's eyes. "I can't believe this is happening. What if they charge her with murder? What if she goes to jail? I wish there were something I could do to help her."

I bit my bottom lip, and Isla gave me a sidelong look. "Rory may be able to help," she said slyly.

Hope sprang to Mira's face. "Really? Do you know Strom?"

I shook my head. "Not at all. What Isla's talking about is that Casey Norton asked me to help investigate this case. I got the feeling she doesn't think Candace did it either, but without some kind of evidence to the contrary, she's their best lead."

"She asked you to help investigate? Like, be a cop or something?"

"A deputy is what she called it. I guess she doesn't have enough people on the payroll who are good at following a trail or something. She thinks I'm good at it—actually, she said I'm nosy—so she asked me for some help."

"You *are* good at being nosy." Mira clapped a hand over her mouth. Through the fingers, she said, muffled, "Sorry. I didn't mean that in a bad way."

I waved it off. "It's cool. I know I'm nosy."

"So, what are you going to do first? Who are you going to question?" Mira looked eager, and the fatigue had lifted from her features.

"Actually, I was thinking about backing out. My mom is after me to do...some stuff at home."

"You can't back out!" Mira grabbed my hands. "Candace can barely afford a lawyer, and a lawyer isn't going to figure out what actually happened anyway. You might be her only hope. I'll help you."

"I'm not sure that's the best idea. After all, if I do it, I'll be the one on payroll, not you. Casey will probably get upset if she finds out you're helping me."

"But you need a helper, right? You could ask her if it could be me."

I hesitated, glancing at Isla, who held up her hands unhelpfully. "Maybe." I drew the word out, not convinced.

"We'll both help you," Isla announced. "And we won't ask Casey for permission. I heard it's easier to ask for forgiveness, anyway. We'll try to lay low, so she doesn't find out we're helping you."

"That doesn't sound like anything that will work at all. In fact, I think it's a pretty good way to get all three of us in a lot of trouble." I hesitated and then smiled. "I like it."

Mira's purse buzzed, and she scrambled to pull out her phone. "It's the police department," she said before answering. "Yes, this is Mira. Okay. Yes, I'll be right there." She slipped the phone off. "I can pick up Candace now. She made bail."

Isla regarded me. "We doing this?"

I only hesitated for a second. "Let's do it. I have to pick up some weird manual from the police department, and I'd like to get a better picture taken. You guys can spring Candace while I do that, then no one will get suspicious that we're working together. I'll meet you back at the Aspen Events office afterward. Bring Candace, so we can talk to her."

"Candace isn't going to want to go to Aspen Events," Mira said. "She was upset about the animals already—they need to be let out and fed. I know she's going to want to go straight to the rescue to do that."

"Okay, I'll meet you there, then. Actually, Jed took my truck, so can you guys drive me to the office now, so I can pick it up?"

"Absolutely." Mira's demeanor was stronger and more determined now that we had a plan to help Candace. Even the bags under her eyes had receded some. "Let's go."

Chapter 4

The Shady Corners animal rescue was housed in a dingy, squat brick building on the edge of town. The grounds were neat, and the building was too, so it was apparent someone took care of it. It was also obvious there wasn't money for large-scale repairs to keep the building up. Some of the bricks were crumbling, and the sidewalk leading up to the front door was missing several chunks.

The front door was locked, but Mira's car was there, so I wandered around the side of the building to see if I could find anyone. The building's back yard was fenced in, and I estimated it to be a couple of acres, with a handful of mature trees closest to the building and a big open area to run and play in the back. Several dogs raced around back there, chasing and jumping at butterflies. I waved when Mira caught sight of me.

She hurried over to unlatch the gate and let me in. "Candace isn't talking about the case. It seems like she's in shock, and she's focusing on what she has to do for the animals. She's inside now, cleaning litter boxes and feeding and watering the cats. Isla and I offered to keep an eye on the dogs out here for her while she did that.

"Will you take me in and introduce me? Then you can come back out while I talk to her. I don't want her to feel overwhelmed with too many people around."

"Good idea." Mira led me to the back door. We were waylaid several times by very good pups coming over to introduce themselves to me and get some head rubs before they bounded off to return to play with their friends. We got through the door and closed it behind us as a giant German shepherd caught sight of me and started to lope his way over. I vowed to say hello to him on my way out.

We followed the sound of metal clinking against metal to find Candace in a small back room working at a waist-high table filled with food bowls. She scooped kibble out of four colorful bags with cat pictures on them to fill the bowls, following a printed list in front of her. She looked at us only briefly before returning to her work.

Mira glanced at me almost apologetically, as though embarrassed her friend wasn't more welcoming, but I waved her off.

"Candace, this is Rory, the person I was telling you about. She's good at figuring things out, and I think she can help you." Mira paused and then added, "She *wants* to help you."

That wasn't entirely true. I mean, sure, if Candace was innocent, I didn't want her to go to jail, but I was supposed to be impartial and figure out the truth no matter what. But it didn't hurt for Candace to think I was on her side. Whatever it took to get her to be forthcoming was fine by me. "Hi. It's nice to meet you. I admire what you're doing here. So many animals need help."

Mira slipped away with a grateful smile cast my way.

Candace said, "Thanks. Somebody has to do it. This is the only no-kill shelter in the county. The more animals I can take in, the more that are saved." She grabbed four bowls in each hand, using her fingers to scrunch them together, and started for the doorway. I scooted aside to let her past. "Grab some bowls and follow me, will ya?"

"Oh. Sure." I went to the table and tried to lift eight bowls like she had, but it was immediately apparent I was not nearly so coordinated and didn't have her finger strength. I didn't want to fumble and cost some kitties any kibble, so I grabbed one bowl in each hand and scurried to follow Candace.

We passed the doorway to the dog kennels. The few who weren't outside yapped at us. Candace said, "Don't worry, you're next," in a soothing tone and continued to a second doorway at the end of the hall.

I followed her into a huge room with floor-to-ceiling cages on three sides. Cats lounged inside on tall trees, cozy beds, or scratching post platforms. When they saw us, many of them made adorable chirping sounds and rubbed on items nearby.

"Aw, they're so cute," I crooned.

"They're the best kitties ever." Candace used the universal sing-songy voice animal-lovers the world over employ as she opened the first cage and stuck in some food bowls. When she turned back to me, she smiled, though it didn't reach her eyes. "I hope you'll excuse my less than friendly behavior—it's not my usual. But today hasn't been a normal day since I don't usually get arrested for murder. I'm glad you're here to try and help me out. Mira says you're great at figuring out mysteries, and I appreciate you trying to help me."

I screwed my lips to the side to once again keep from saying I wasn't necessarily there specifically to help her. It was my job to figure out what happened to Strom, not necessarily to clear Candace. "The victim was the shelter's landlord?"

She nodded and watched a couple cats come to their bowls and begin to eat before heading for the doorway again.

I followed her, figuring the only way I was going to have a conversation with this woman was if I helped her care for the animals.

"He was, but I was about to lose my lease."

"Lose it? You mean Strom was going to kick you and the animals out of this building?" I could only imagine how much heartache that would cause Candace. It was clear she was as devoted to her work as anyone could be.

After retrieving the rest of the bowls from the supply room, Candace paused in the hallway. "Yep. I'm about a week late on the rent. I have no doubt he would have been here serving eviction papers if I wasn't able to hand him a check this afternoon."

This afternoon? She wasn't kidding when she said she was about to lose the lease.

Candace continued, moving past me with her bowls. "I was praying we would make enough at the fun run today to cover what I owe. Maybe even to get ahead a few months to give me some time to breathe and figure out how to get some more steady income. Turns out, it was enough to post my bail, and now I have to pay that money back to the shelter somehow."

I leaned against the doorway to the cat room to watch her deliver the final bowls, considering what she had said. "How *do* you make money for this place?"

She relatched the cage and wiped her hands on her jeans. "Donations, mainly. Once in a while, I'm able to get grant money, but that's only a little and pretty far between because I don't have time to research and write all the proposals. Plus, I don't have expertise in that, either. What I need is an endowment, not that I want anyone to die. Anyway, I can't count on that anytime soon, so I need to figure out what to do."

"Can you move to another building? With a different landlord?"

"I've considered it, and I've gone to look at every place that's come up for rent in the last year, but nothing's been right. We need a pretty particular set-up here, with room for the dogs to run and a big, airy, sunny area for the cats." She waved a hand toward the room we had exited. "This is a pretty special place, though it needs a lot of upkeep that I can't afford, and Strom wouldn't do it. The plumbing is desperate for an upgrade, and the fuse box is a nightmare. If I run the dishwasher and the microwave at the same time, something makes a sizzling sound, and the fuse blows."

"Yikes, that sounds like a fire hazard or something. Doesn't your landlord *have* to deal with things like that?"

Candace moved down a hallway I hadn't seen before, jutting toward the front of the building, and I followed. "Strom had a lot of people in this town in his back pocket," she explained over her shoulder. "I guess city inspectors must've been on the list. I'm not sure, but that's what I suspect, anyway. We got notices that the electric needed to be upgraded, but no one ever came to insist on it. I don't know if he got fined or anything like that, but I don't suspect so. Strom wasn't known for wasting money on things like fees and fines."

"Do you know what happens to the building now? Who will be your new landlord?" We'd entered a big room with small cages lining two walls. I realized this was where the small animals were—gerbils, hamsters, and rabbits. "Oh! Is that a chinchilla?" I hurried to the cage to peek in on the furry ball snoozing in the corner.

"Her name's Bella. You in the market for a 'chilla?"

"No way, but Isla said she may be. I'll have to tell her Bella's here." I turned away, but a bunny hopped to the front of the cage to Bella's left. When we made eye contact, it almost seemed to have human-like sentience behind its eyes. I blinked rapidly a few times, startled as it seemed to look right through me. I had to struggle to bring my attention back to what Candace was saying.

"Linda Pearson may take over as my landlord, I guess. I'm not sure."

"Strom's wife?" I thought of the poor woman who'd thrown herself on the victim's lifeless body. It made sense she'd be the landlord now.

I cut my eyes to the bunny again. It still sat at the front of the cage, staring unblinkingly at me. *Creepy.*

Candace gave me an odd look. "Yes, his wife. Like I said, I'm not sure. I don't think there was anything in my contract about what happened if Strom was killed or died or whatever. But Linda came around a time or two with Strom when he visited or came threatening to close me down if I didn't come up with some money."

I couldn't tear my gaze away from the bunny, but I asked, "Did she seem to feel the same way he did about your lease?"

Candace tossed some new cedar chips into a hamster cage for bedding. "She didn't argue with him. She seemed to hate it here—I don't think she likes animals. But she never said anything one way or the other." Candace came over to stand beside me and directed her eyes where mine looked. "Are you in the market for adopting a bunny?"

"What? Adopt? Me? No. I have a dog already. And a cat. I don't know anything about rabbits. No."

Candace raised an eyebrow. "Okay. You look interested in Stuart. And, um, he looks interested in you too." Her brow wrinkled in confusion. "Do you want me to get him out, so you can visit with him?"

"No." I said it before I had a chance to think. Then my jaw dropped when the bunny gave me a recriminating look. "Actually, I do want him." What was happening? Why did I say that? "What do you need to have to take care of a rabbit?" Why was my mouth working independently of my brain? I did *not* want to take Stuart home.

"A cage, some bedding, some rabbit pellets. You have to add fresh veggies to his meals. I don't adopt out bunnies if people are planning to keep them outside. It's too dangerous out there—they can get eaten by coyotes and stray dogs. Oh, and he needs plenty of fresh water at all times, and he'll make a mess of it on the regular, so it needs to be changed like four times a day unless you get a hanging water bottle."

I most certainly didn't want to deal with having a rabbit, especially since I'd never had one before and had no idea how to care for one. But Stuart *was* giving me the eye, and I couldn't help but think something was odd about him. I had an overwhelming urge to take him home, even as my practical side screamed against it. "Okay, yes. I wouldn't keep him outside and I'll get a water bottle. We always have lots of veggies around the house."

"You can have him, then. Usually, there's a screening process, but I can't be too choosy right now. I may be in jail soon, or I could lose this place, and all the animals will have to go to kill shelters if either of those things happen. So, you can have him and any other animals you feel like adopting right this second. In fact, I have a cage you can have for him, and I'll give you enough rabbit pellets to get you through a week or two while you settle him in."

"Great. Do you have, like, a rabbit care manual or something like that? I'm a complete newbie." I could keep it with my deputy manual, which I hadn't read a word of before questioning Candace.

She smirked. "I have some standard paperwork I give everyone who adopts a rabbit. It should have everything you need to get started, and you'll want to make an appointment right away with Dr. Arlington-Sands."

"Oh, she's my vet already. For my German shorthaired pointer, Piper."

Candace didn't seem to care about that because she didn't answer me. Instead, she set about gathering items out of a closet.

Tearing my eyes away from the strange rabbit, who I was about to own against my better judgment, I asked, "Did you load the dye gun that killed Strom Pearson?"

She slid her eyes to me over her shoulder before refocusing on the closet. "I loaded it before I left here this morning and one more time when it ran out of dye during the race. But my friend, Roger, loaded it the last time."

She had all my attention at that, the rabbit forgotten. "Roger? The caterer?"

Nodding, she closed the closet door and handed me a bag full of rabbit accoutrements. "That's him. You know him?" She gave her head a tiny shake. "Of course you do. You're an event planner. Plus, Mira works for you."

"Yeah, he's done some catering for me in the past. And because of Mira." I didn't add that I'd used a tiny touch of Valentine's Day magic to nudge the two off on their first date. They'd been super interested in each other, but neither was making the first move. I was like a matchmaker who couldn't take credit for it.

She crossed her arms and cocked a hip. "The two of them are nice together. I'm rooting for them."

"Did you watch Roger load the dye gun?"

She gave that some thought. "No. Mrs. Anderson came up and asked me about Lulu. That's a border collie we have up for adoption. That's why Roger offered to load the gun—he said he knew how from playing paintball—and I didn't pay any attention while he did it."

That was interesting. How was I going to explain to Mira that I needed to question her boyfriend about the murder? She'd already been so upset about Candace, I could imagine the stricken look on her face when I told her about Roger.

I tailed Candace to the lobby, where she had me sign some paperwork and then handed me the cage containing Stuart. "Normally, I'd tell you to call me if you have any questions, but I have no idea where I'll be or in what state of mind. So, I'd suggest you call Dr. Arlington-Sands if you need something." She sank onto an office chair and blew out a breath, suddenly looking exhausted. "I can't believe this happened. I don't know what I'm going to do." She grabbed a stack of mail and flipped through it, seemed disappointed, and tossed it in the trash.

"Do you have a lawyer?"

Candace shook her head. "Mira and Roger were telling me I should get one, even before this. To fight Strom if I needed to. But I don't have the money." She looked at the ceiling, and I followed her gaze. There were watermarks on all the corner tiles. "I've sunk everything I have into this place. There's nothing left. I mean, it's not like I ever expected to do all that great financially. I run a nonprofit for a living, after all."

"Where do you get your money for your own life? To live on, I mean."

She snorted. "I have a part-time job at the grocery store. I ring up groceries, and sometimes I fill in for a bagger. It's not a lot, but it's enough to pay for a crappy apartment on the other side of town and for gas in my car and insurance. I live with my mom, and she pays for utilities and sometimes part of the rent with her pension and social security money. She pays for most of our food too. Sometimes, I have to use some of my grocery pay to cover the lease on this place, and then we get behind on the apartment. The landlord over there is a lot more easy-going, though, and she's an animal lover, so she always lets us slide. You know, Strom tried to buy her buildings from her—she only has two. I'm glad she resisted and didn't give them up. There aren't a lot of other landlords in this town because Strom tried to create a monopoly, so he could control the rent."

"That doesn't sound legal."

She grunted. "Small town, small rules. There wasn't anyone challenging him. I mean, if someone wanted to hire a fancy lawyer from the big city, they could have, but no one has the money or the gumption, I guess. I can only hope that Linda Pearson, if she's the one who's inheriting Strom's properties, has more of a heart than he did. But I wouldn't bet the farm on it."

"Okay, I'm going to get out of here and do some more investigating. But if there's any way you can afford a lawyer, I strongly advise you to get one." I hefted Stuart's cage in one hand and his bag of stuff in the other.

Candace let me out the front of the building and said she'd send Mira and Isla around from the back. She didn't want the dogs to frighten the bunny in my hand. I sent a silent sorry to the German shepherd. I was going to have to break my promise to him. I turned to Candace. "Hey, show Bella to Isla, okay? You may be able to get another animal homed."

She nodded and locked the door behind me.

As I waited by my truck, I peered into the cage at Stuart. "I hope you're happy. I mean, I *seriously* hope you're happy because I have no idea what makes bunnies happy."

"I don't know what makes bunnies happy either," he replied. "But I do know it took you long enough to find me."

Chapter 5

It was past lunchtime, and Isla needed to get back to finish up some cooking for a catering event that evening. And to get Bella settled in her new home. Candace had given her a cage and some supplies too, and the chinchilla blinked sleepily at us from a tiny pink bed.

"I'll drive you, Isla," Mira offered. Then she turned to me. "Who's next on your list of people to question?"

I hesitated, considering telling her a white lie, but I knew it was only a matter of time before she found out anyway. I'd rather tell her myself. "I need to talk to Roger."

"Roger? My Roger? I mean, he's not mine. He's his own Roger. But he's my boyfriend. Or the guy I'm dating. Or something. I guess." She stuttered to a halt. After a deep breath, she started again. "You need to question Roger about Strom's murder?"

"Candace told me Roger reloaded the dye gun right before she shot it at Strom. So, I need to talk to him. I think I should do it alone. Without you, I mean. I have to take this bunny home and get him settled first."

Both women blinked at the cage at my feet. Then Isla squealed and knelt to peer in. "You adopted a bunny? Why did you do that? Oh, he's so cute and fluffy." She gasped and craned to peer up at me. "He can play with Bella!"

I regarded Stuart. Isla was right that he was adorable, with wispy brown and white fur that looked as though it could be almost too soft to believe. His long ears flopped adorably to the sides, and a white patch on the right side of his face resembled a crooked heart.

"I guess so."

"You don't sound thrilled about it. Why'd you adopt him if you didn't want a rabbit?" Isla stuck her finger through the bars, and Stuart sniffed at it, making her squeal in adoration again.

"I'm not sure. It's a long story. But I have to take him home and get him settled, and then I'm going to go talk to Roger. I'll call you guys later and let you know what happened, okay?" To Mira, I said, "It's going to be okay. I'm sure Roger will have some information for me that will send me along to the next person."

"I sure hope so. Thanks, Rory."

I watched Mira and Isla, with Bella's cage in hand, climb into Mira's car and leave. I hoisted Stuart's cage onto the passenger seat of my truck.

The bunny sniffed and then drew his lips back from his giant buck teeth. "It smells funny in here."

"What are you talking about? It smells like me. And coffee."

"Smells like a canine," he said before sneezing five times. Adorable sneezes but alarming.

"You're not sick, are you?" I didn't know anything about sick bunnies, and his sneezes concerned me. In the back of my mind, I knew I should probably be more alarmed that he was talking to me than that he was sneezing. *Details.*

"Dog odor is appalling." His voice was much lower than you would expect from a bunny. Not that you would expect any voice from a bunny—I certainly didn't. But, at any rate, it was lower than it seemed like a voice should be for the size and adorability factor that Stuart possessed.

"You're probably smelling my dog, Piper. You'll be meeting her soon."

"I have to live with a dog?" He made a noise that sounded like a bark of wry laughter. "The universe has it in for me these days."

"Hold that thought." I closed the door, ran around, and climbed in the driver's side. As I was putting on my seatbelt, I said, "The universe, huh? So, does that mean you're saying you were sent here or something?"

"Of course, I was. Why would I be here otherwise? I don't want to live with a dog. Filthy, drooly creatures."

"Piper isn't filthy." I felt outraged on her behalf. "She's very clean, and she also doesn't drool unless she finds a good smell out in the woods. You won't be out in the woods with her when she finds a good smell, so I think you're safe."

"Are you saying this canine is a hunting dog?" Stuart sounded flabbergasted and a little scared.

"No, she isn't. I mean, she could be, but we've never trained her to do that. We aren't hunters."

A little shudder went through the bunny's whole body, and relief flooded his voice. "Thank goodness. Still, I think I'd like to be kept good and separate from this canine. What if she thinks I'm a chew toy or something?"

"She'll probably be pretty excited when you two first meet, but Piper will obey us if we tell her to leave you alone. And she isn't going to think you're a chew toy. She's not stupid. She knows the difference between a living thing and a piece of rubber. Besides, this isn't what I want to talk to you about right now. I mean, since we're talking, which is completely weird. What I want to know is why you're here. *Why* you're talking to me."

"I thought that would be obvious. But Sasha did tell our supervisors you are not the brightest witch in the coven."

Understanding slammed through me. "You're my new familiar." Sasha, my mother's familiar, had told me I would be getting one of my own. I'd expected a cat, even though she had told me it could be lots of other animals. A rabbit had never occurred to me.

"Ah. You've caught on. Thank goodness. Now I can have a nap." He settled back on his haunches.

"It won't take us long to get home. You don't need a nap. I have to go out again soon, and you can rest then. For now, I want you to tell me why your supervisors or whatever think I need my own familiar. Sasha is enough to handle." I said the last part under my breath.

Apparently, rabbits have excellent hearing. At least rabbits who are familiars, which, as near as I could figure, means they're an ancient person's spirit in an animal's body. "Sasha is a top-level familiar, and you've been lucky to have her. But she's been doing double duty, and she doesn't need to. You've reached the point in your abilities when a familiar is always designated. Your mother declined one on your behalf years ago, but you weren't ready then anyway." He yawned, giving me a great view of his cute little bunny mouth. "Besides, with the situation you're in with Xavier, it was decided that you need a real, bonded familiar. One you can hear in your mind, so they can be around and talk to you while other people are in the area."

I had started to back the truck up, but now I stepped on the brakes and slammed it back into park so I could turn toward him. "Did you say you can talk to me in my mind?"

"Of course, I can. Same as Sasha can talk into your mother's mind."

"She can?"

"Yes. She only talks out loud when you're around out of respect for you. Though I imagine she says additional things telepathically to her. Likely complaints about your ability to reason." He pinned me with that mildly creepy stare. "Or lack thereof."

"Why did no one tell me this? This is something I would liked to have known."

Stuart bobbed his head in a good impression of a human shrug. "I don't make the rules, nor do I make the decisions. As evidenced by the fact that I'm in a cage in the cab of a stinky pickup truck heading to my life as a dog's roommate." He lay down, turned his head away, and refused to respond when I called his name again.

I threw the truck into drive and grumbled all the way home about annoying, uncooperative familiars.

Stuart didn't even twitch an ear tip.

Chapter 6

There was much oohing and aahing over Stuart when I got home. To my slight irritation, he was adorable and goofy with my family. Mom and Dad both loved him, instantly pulling him out of the crate and getting in some snuggle time. Sasha wasn't at all surprised to see him, and they greeted each other affectionately.

I made a beeline for Piper, grabbing her around the middle and sitting on the floor to let her curl up in my lap for a few minutes, keeping her calm while she got used to the scent and sight of Stuart. The rabbit eyed the dog up at first but eventually ignored her, apparently comfortable she wouldn't attack him.

When I did let the Piper go, she used her manners quite well, much to my pride. She gave Stuart a tiny sniff and an even tinier lick. Then she lay down with her chin on her paws, only her eager eyes showing that she wanted to play with the bunny.

After half an hour of getting acquainted and eating a quick sandwich, I smacked my hands on the table and got to my feet. "Okay, I have to get going. I need to talk to someone about Strom's murder."

"Yes, let's go, then." Stuart hopped off my mom's lap onto the floor.

I blinked. "You can't come with me."

"Why not?"

"Because you're a...well, you're a rabbit. How am I going to take you into a catering business to ask someone questions?"

"That isn't any of my concern. What's my concern is that I stay with you and help as needed. That's my task, not figuring out how to get by in the human world." He tipped his head, and the heart-shaped mark on his face became more well-defined.

"She's always worried about this type of thing," Sasha offered.

"Seems rather tiresome. I can see why you're glad to get rid of her." Stuart shook his head, and I wasn't sure if he was being condescending or had some type of a problem. I hoped there was a section on ear care in the rabbit care manual Candace had given me.

Great. Now I had two important manuals and no time to read either one.

"I've gotten used to Aurora," Sasha said with a bored tone. "You probably will too, though it takes a few weeks, at least. She can be quite bumbling and often forgets to use magic when she can or should, so you'll find yourself reminding her a lot. But she has a good heart, like her mother."

"Aw! You're so sweet. You have a good heart too." Mom knelt to rub the sides of Sasha's cheeks.

Stuart snuffled. "A witch who forgets to use her magic? Classic. I was the familiar for a wizard who was like that back in the 1300s. Eventually, he forgot one too many times and got fried by an angry witch he had two-timed like an idiot."

"I'm not going to two-time anyone, so you won't have to worry about that." I felt disgruntled that the familiars were talking about me as though I wasn't there. And as though I were inept. "Look, I have to go before it gets too late for me to talk to this person. Stuart, I guess if you insist on coming along, you'll have to find your own way. You can do that, right?" I assumed he was like Sasha, who seemed to be able to transport herself or something. Even when I left her at home and didn't share where I was going, she always showed up where I was. I never knew how she managed to track me down or move so fast.

"I can, but it's disrespectful of you to leave me and take off on your own. I should be with you at all times, and you should carry me." He wrinkled his nose like he'd smelled a rotten carrot.

Frustration rolled through me. "I can't carry a bunny around with me everywhere. People will think I'm nuts, and then they won't answer my questions."

"Why would people think you're crazy for carrying a rabbit? People carry those tiny little dogs in their purses everywhere."

"You're not helping, Dad." I gave him a stern look.

He held up his hands in surrender. "Sorry. I'm only saying you have that big tote bag you carry around a lot. Your familiar could go in there."

I cocked my jaw and gave it some thought. It wasn't a terrible idea. I did carry the tote a lot, so people in town were used to seeing me with it. Plus, I'd be sure to have the stuff I needed on me all the time, assuming Stuart could be happy hanging out with a few extra lipsticks, some sunglasses, and a notepad and pen. "Fine. I'll grab the tote. But you can't stick your furry head out when I'm talking to people, and you have to let me know if you need to go to the bathroom. I can't have rabbit poop all over my stuff—plus, it'll ruin the bag."

Stuart sat up on his haunches, as though he were getting ready to box someone. "Are you seriously suggesting I would relieve myself inside of a purse? I've never had my honor so maligned by a witch or wizard before." He shook his head and dropped back onto his front paws. "You have a lot to learn, Missy."

I pulled a breath through my nose and counted to seven. I'd aimed for ten but lost patience. "My name is Rory, and I'd appreciate it if you used it. Sasha calls me Aurora, and I can deal with that too. I'm sorry I offended you. I'll try not to do it again, and I'd appreciate it if you gave me some respect too. I may be a witch, but I'm not an idiot."

Sasha cocked her head, as though planning to take issue with what I'd said, but she kept her kitty lips shut.

I stomped out of the kitchen and up the stairs to my bedroom, where I pawed through the closet until I found the beige tote with black stars that I loved so much. I stuffed some supplies into it and tromped back down the steps. I dropped the tote on the floor next to Stuart. "Okay, climb in. Let's go."

Thankfully, Stuart hopped in without another word.

Maybe I was getting somewhere with these familiars.

LIVING IN SHADY CORNERS was sort of a novelty—my truck was so old because I barely put any miles on it. I walked a lot of places, even in the winter. So, driving to the next town over to visit Roger was more exciting than it probably should have been. It was fun to see different scenery and was even a nice enough day for me to lower the windows and turn up the radio.

It wasn't until I was almost there that I realized I probably should have saved this particular errand for the next day because it was already late afternoon. The events of that morning seemed like they'd taken place days ago. When I'd woken up, I certainly hadn't expected to be on the police department's payroll and carting around a new familiar by the end of the day, my business in even more trouble than it had been.

I shoved the thought aside. There was nothing I could do about that except try to find Strom's killer and prove my business had nothing to do with it.

Again.

The building Roger rented for his catering business was only barely in better shape than the animal shelter, another single-level brick building. The grounds were in better shape, with no broken sidewalk leading up to it, though, and I went in the front door, greeted by the tinkling of bells. I adjusted the tote on my shoulder. "You're heavier than you look, rabbit," I mumbled under my breath. In response, Stuart pitched his weight suddenly, causing me to have to do a little two-step to resist falling on my behind. "Knock it off."

"Knock what off?" Roger emerged from a back room looking puzzled, but he smiled broadly when he saw me. "Rory, I didn't expect to see you. With as busy a day as you've had, I figured you'd be in bed already or something. What's up? Got an event Isla can't cover?"

Isla handled the catering for ninety percent of my events that required food. On the rare times when she couldn't, Mira usually called Roger.

For the part of the ride over when I hadn't been singing at the top of my lungs, I had given some consideration about how to explain to Roger why I was coming around to ask questions. I'd rolled a few different excuses over in my mind but decided against all of them. "Casey Norton hired me to look into what happened to Strom Pearson," I said evenly.

He grabbed a spray bottle and cloth and got to work cleaning the counter. "Wow. That's big time. I thought you pretty much had your hands full with Aspen Events."

I didn't answer but looked around the lobby. Three small round tables with chairs around them took up most of the space in the open part of the room. A long counter interrupted by a swinging half door stood against the far wall with the doorway to the kitchen, and framed pictures of food hung at intervals on the walls. "This place looks nice," I said. "I should totally get some artwork up at my office. And, to answer your question, yes, the business keeps me busy, but Mira has been taking over more and more of the responsibility, as I'm sure you know." I grinned.

Roger chuckled. "I do know that. I also know Mira loves doing it. She's happy working for you."

"That's good to hear from someone other than her. I don't know what I would do without her. Therefore, it's my goal to keep her as happy as humanly possible."

He cocked his head. "So, you're here in your role as investigator, then? What do you want to ask me?"

I set the tote bag on a nearby chair and felt Stuart readjust himself inside. Roger's eyes dropped to the tote and narrowed, as though he'd seen the movement. To cover up and hopefully take his mind off it, I launched in. "Did you swap out the dye canister for Candace right before she shot it at Strom?"

He pursed his lips for a second, regarding me, and then said, "I did. She was busy talking to someone, and she asked me to."

"How did you know how to do it? I don't think I would have if she'd asked me."

"It works like the paintball guns I used to play with as a teenager. The canisters are a little different, that's all. She asked me if I knew how to do it, and I said I did."

"I see. And where did you get the canister to replace the used one from?"

"There was a box in Candace's hatch. Two boxes, actually. One was full of old canisters, and the other one had a new one. I grabbed it, stuck it in the gun, and carried it back over to the finish line."

"Grabbed it? There was only one new canister there?"

Roger nodded. "Yep. I assumed it was the box that held purple canisters. Purple was what Candace was using at the finish line. I figured the other volunteers had their own boxes of new canisters in their color at each of their stations. There was also a box with a bunch of empty, used canisters."

"How many?"

A frown pulled down the corners of his mouth. "Actually, it was pretty full. Like a dozen?"

"But surely, she hadn't used a dozen canisters of purple paint at the finish line already?"

Roger's brow scrunched into wrinkles as he thought about it. "I wouldn't think so. There could have been a runner bringing used canisters to Candace's car from the other stations. I never gave it any thought. Didn't notice if the used ones were all one color or a bunch of different ones." His tone told me he was giving it some thought now, and it wasn't adding up, like it hadn't for me.

"How well did you know Strom?" I filed away the inconsistency about canisters to think on later.

"Not well. He came around once in a while to look at the place." He gestured at the building around us. "Sometimes he dropped in to tell me he'd jacked up the rent, like the last time I saw him."

"When was that?"

"A couple days ago. He and his wife stopped by. I tried to get him to look at the leaky faucet in the bathroom in the back." He jerked his head toward the room he'd emerged from. "He ignored me about that, of course—he never fixed a single broken thing around here. Then he told me the rent was going up by a hundred dollars a month, effective next time it was due."

"That doesn't seem right. He didn't give you any notice at all? That seems like a big increase."

"Nope. But that was nothing new. He never gave me much notice."

"So, he'd done this before? How often did he raise the rent on you?"

Roger scrunched his nose and looked up at the ceiling as though filing through memories. "I couldn't tell you exactly, but I guess half a dozen?"

"Wow. Over what time period was that?"

"I've been in this building for about four years. Of course, I keep thinking about finding another place under a different landlord, but I'd have to move even farther away for that. And now that Mira and I are dating, I don't want to have a longer drive to Shady Corners."

I grinned. "I'm so glad you and Mira are doing well. She's been super happy lately."

"I'm the clear winner in this game," he insisted. "She's too good for me, but she doesn't know that yet. I'm going to try and keep her from figuring it out for as long as I possibly can. By then, I hope to have earned enough of her good will to keep her around."

I laughed and grabbed the handles of my tote bag. "Who do you think is going to be your landlord now? Do you have any idea?"

"Not really. I was thinking about pulling out my contract and seeing if it had a clause about what happens in the event of the landlord's death. Strom's lawyers were always real good—they never left any wiggle room for anything to happen that didn't benefit him. At least, I don't think they did. I didn't have the money to hire my own lawyer, so it was a matter of me scouring the legalese myself. But I hope it's someone better than him. Probably, it'll be Linda."

"Strom's wife? Do you think she'll be better than he was?"

He paused for a moment and then shook his head. "I couldn't say. She never said much of anything when she was here with him. But I got the feeling she was taking in everything he did. Learning his methods, so to speak. So, I'm not going to get my hopes up that she'll lower my rent or even keep it where it is. Probably won't spring to fix anything around here either. I've gotten to be good friends with a plumber, an electrician, and a landscaper, so I can handle the upkeep on this place myself without breaking the bank too much. It's a shame. Those contractors deserve more than I can pay them for what they do around here. I keep hoping I'll make it big someday and be able to pay them back."

I thought about the animal shelter. Candace's testimony about Strom and living under his lease paralleled Roger's in so many ways. "You can handle the new rent amount, though? Without being at risk of your business going under, I mean?"

"Yeah, I can handle it. It means less take-home pay for me, which isn't great, but it's part of running a business. Luckily, I live pretty simply. I have a studio apartment over by the river." He jabbed a finger in the direction he meant. "I don't bring Mira to it because it's pretty humble, but it's a safe roof over my head, and I'm not there much anyway."

"Spending most of your time here, huh?"

"Yep. Either I'm working on a catering order or trying new recipes to offer people, or I am working on figuring out cheaper ways to advertise and gain new clients. I have my eye on a commercial kitchen over in Canton. That's equidistant from Shady Corners and here, and that place has a different landlord. But it's an extra thousand in rent per month, so I need to beef up my bottom line before I can even consider it. Still, that's the long-term goal, but, of course, I'll have to cross my fingers and hope the place is still available once I'm able to afford it."

I hoisted the tote onto my shoulder. "I hope you can do it sooner rather than later. Thanks for answering my questions." I headed for the door but stopped and turned back toward him. "Did you kill Strom Pearson?"

He didn't answer for so long I started to get worried, but finally, he shook his head. "Nope. But I can't say I'm sorry he's dead."

Chapter 7

Halfway back to Shady Corners, the buzz of my cell phone interrupted my train of thought. I'd been deep into reviewing and analyzing what Roger had said. I grabbed the phone and, seeing that it was Isla calling, swiped to answer.

Without saying hello, she launched right in. "How about a double date tonight?"

"Oh, I don't know, girl. I'm pretty tired." As though to drive the words home, exhaustion flooded through my shoulders, making them ache. It *had* been a long day.

"Did you eat yet? Dinner?"

"No."

"You have to eat dinner. Might as well be with your gorgeous boyfriend and equally attractive best friend, right?"

With a groan, I turned the steering wheel and started on the last leg of road toward Shady Corners. "I guess so." It would be nice to see Cam, though I didn't even know if he was available.

As though she read my mind, Isla said, "I already talked to Cam. He's game if you are."

"Do I have to dress up?"

"We're going to get burgers, so no. You don't."

Just then, something occurred to me. "Did you say you called my boyfriend before you called me about going out tonight?"

"I had a feeling you'd try to dodge, so I figured I'd handle any objections before you had a chance to make them." Laughter was evident in her tone. "Where are you? Can you be at my place in ten minutes?"

Stuart stuck his head out of the tote. "I would much rather go back to your modest home, have some dinner, and retire to my own cage."

"Duly noted," I told him.

"What?" Isla said.

"Nothing. I guess I can be there in about ten minutes. Is Cam going to meet us at the restaurant?"

"No, he's coming to my place too."

"Okay, I'll see you soon."

We hung up, and I stared straight forward, avoiding Stuart's glare. How does a rabbit glare anyway? I wasn't sure, but he managed it fine. More than fine. "I'll drop you off at home if you want me to," I offered.

"You know I need to be with you all the time. Xavier could strike at any moment."

"Yeah, so I keep being told. But yet, nothing ever happens." I slowed down to twenty-five miles per hour as the truck rolled into the city limits.

"It's only a matter of time."

"So you all say." Mom and Sasha had been insisting Xavier was close since Valentine's Day. In fact, they'd claimed he was on his way at that time, and we needed to go on the run—take off from Shady Corners and head into hiding. Live like nomads trying to stay one step ahead of the wizard. I'd refused, and Xavier had not shown up.

In exchange for insisting we stay in town, I'd agreed to a hefty training regimen with my mom and Sasha. We'd gone to Alaska for two weeks, and during that time, I learned a lot about my ability to wield magic. I could easily tap into energy webs that were not related to holidays now, and I was feeling proficient after a couple of months of study. But nothing further had happened with Xavier, and I was starting to doubt that he was actually after me.

Stuart ignored my grumbling and settled back into the tote. "The least you could do is pass a few morsels from your dinner into this horrible, cramped bag."

"I'll see what I can do, but I have no idea what's safe to feed rabbits and what isn't."

"Throw stuff in. If I'm not supposed to eat it, I'll leave it for you to clean up later."

"That sounds...disgusting."

"Then let's skip dinner out and head back to your house," he suggested with a righteous tone.

I clamped my lips together to keep from sniping back and drove the rest the way in silence.

The minute I stepped into Isla's house, Stuart in his tote over my shoulder, I felt strange. I couldn't put my finger on what was going on as I slipped off my shoes and padded down the hallway toward the kitchen, where I could hear voices. The minute I stepped through the doorway, I knew what it was.

Isla sat at the bar with a glass of wine in front of her, talking to a man I knew. "Lance. What are you doing back here?"

The dark-haired man turned toward me and delivered a bright smile. "Rory. It's great to see you again. I came up to see Isla. I was hoping to convince her to go out with me and am happy to report she agreed." He turned his attention back to her. "Of course, she insisted on our first date being a double. You can't blame her—a girl has to be safe."

Isla shook her head. "I'm not trying to be safe. I'm trying to make sure we don't have some weird, awkward lull in the conversation by including two other people who can talk if we run out of subjects. You know, keep everything from being all first-datey." She grimaced as though a first date was the worst possible event in the world.

"I'm sorry, I'm still not following. I thought you were trying to get Isla to move to Ann Arbor and be the executive chef at your fancy restaurant. She said no, and you left. That's not what you're here for this time?"

When Lance had come to Shady Corners in February, he and Isla had snuck around having business meetings. I thought she was dating someone she didn't want to introduce me to, and it had caused some hard feelings. But it turned out she was afraid to tell me she was thinking about moving downstate to Ann Arbor and taking the new position. That hurt my feelings too, since I thought we talked about everything. Ultimately, she'd decided against going, much to my joy, and Lance had left, much to my appreciation. I'd shoved away the hurt feelings and moved on.

It wasn't that I didn't like the guy—I didn't have any reason to like *or* dislike him, having only met him once briefly on a sidewalk while I wore a fancy gown. But I got an odd feeling from him that I couldn't my finger on.

"Nope. I'm not here for business this time. I'm here for pure pleasure."

I was hit with a gag reflex so strong I had to put a hand to my throat to calm it down. *Gross.* I opened my mouth to answer, having no idea what to say, and was thankfully spared by the sound of the front door opening and closing. "Oh, I'll bet that's Cam." I leaned backward to get line of sight with the front door and, sure enough, saw my boyfriend taking his shoes off. "Yep. Here he is." My voice was too high-pitched.

I glanced at Isla, and her eyes were slightly narrowed. She was onto me. There was no way I could ever hide anything from her. That's why she'd known about my witch-related secrets from the very beginning, since we were both toddlers. I gave her an apologetic smile. I wasn't trying to feel weird about Lance—it wasn't my fault.

As Cam approached, a voice echoed in my mind. Someone else's, not my own. *I don't trust that guy. You shouldn't either.*

I stiffened. I glanced around, but no one else had heard.

There's something off about him.

It hit me the voice was Stuart's. Inside my mind. I remembered what he'd said about me being assigned a familiar who could communicate telepathically with me.

Um. Okay. I had no idea if I'd broadcast that thought to him or not.

Cam gave me a peck on the cheek and a squeeze around the shoulders. "Glad you could make it. I didn't expect to see you for a second time today."

I smiled and reached up to fluff his hair. "You missed a little purple."

His eyes widened. "I did? I swear I spent twenty minutes in the shower trying to scrub off every last bit of dye."

"That's okay, it's cute. Maybe you should keep it."

He gave me another kiss. "I'll let you be the one with colorful hair in our relationship. It suits you better." His gaze moved into the kitchen. "Oh, hi there. I'm Cam."

"Lance. It's nice to meet you. Isla tells me you're the best server she has."

Cam ducked his head. "I have a lot of experience waiting tables. I like serving at events, though. It's different and a lot of fun."

"Plus, you often get to wear a tux, and then you're even hotter than usual," I put in, trying to ignore the rabbit shifting his weight in my tote.

You have a bony hip.

"I'll be right back!" I hurried away, up the stairs to Isla's bedroom. I went in, closed the door, and dumped my familiar onto the bed. "You're talking in my mind. It's freaking me out."

He cocked his head, sending a long ear to flopping adorably. *I'm your familiar, so...*

"Right. My familiar. So, I guess I'll have to get used to talking in my mind and try not to be freaked out." I flopped onto the bed next to him and absently scratched his ears.

Stuart leaned into it. "I'm your familiar. We are bonded. It won't take you long to get used to."

I tipped my head. "How do I make you hear me?"

"Think normally but direct the thought toward me when you wish me to hear it."

That sounded easy. *Like this?*

He blinked at me and didn't answer.

Stuart, can you hear me?

Another blink and total silence.

I wasn't very good at this.

Then something flitted across his face. I don't know how I noticed—his bunny features didn't have a lot of ability for expression. It was something in the eyes.

I arched a brow. *You look like a plumper version of the Velveteen rabbit, only less loved and more crumpled.*

Hey! In my mind, it was a shout.

You can hear me!

He chuckled and spoke out loud. "I was only razzing you." He looked around. "This is a dump."

The bedspread was crumpled, and the top sheet had fallen to the floor, where it lay among piles of clothing. Probably, even Isla didn't know what was clean or dirty. "She's busy with her business. She doesn't have time for too much housework. Actually, she keeps the main level pretty good because clients are sometimes down there, but the second level, she lets go of." I wrinkled my nose. "You don't want to see the bathroom."

"I'd rather be inside that cramped tote. Please take me back downstairs."

With a chuckle, I complied, glad Stuart and I finally found something to agree on. I started to leave the room but then paused and peered into the bag at my familiar. "Wait a second, you said you don't trust Lance. Why not?"

"I'm not sure. There's something about him that's...off. I can't place it, but I know you should keep him at arms' length."

"You don't have to tell me twice. In fact, you didn't have to tell me once. I got the same vibe from him."

"It's good to hear you're trusting your witchy senses. I wasn't sure you had any."

"How can you turn our agreeing on something into a jab at me?"

"It's a particular talent I have." I could hear the grin in his voice even though his rabbit features didn't make one.

I rolled my eyes. "Fine. By the way, keep telling me stuff like that. In case my witchy senses suffer a short or something."

"That *is* my job."

"Yeah, yeah." I scooted back downstairs. "Okay, all set. Sorry about the delay."

"No problem. We were discussing wine. Let's walk to the restaurant, okay?" Isla got to her feet and linked an arm through mine, leading me out to the foyer ahead of the guys. She leaned in to whisper, "Lance totally surprised me. Showed up at my door out of nowhere and asked me out. It's kind of romantic."

"Or a little stalker-ish?" I suggested.

She winked at me. "Hence the double date."

I rolled my eyes. "I thought that was so there wouldn't be awkward pauses in the conversation."

With a shrug, she opened the door. "Awkward pauses are especially problematic if you're with a stalker."

DINNER WENT FINE. I kept watch Lance while trying not to make it obvious I was doing so. He seemed to only have eyes for Isla, keeping his attention on her unless he absolutely had to engage with me or Cam.

I didn't talk much. Between fatigue and uneasiness about Lance, I wasn't in a chatty mood, and that drew a few glares from my best friend. I gave her helpless shrugs in return and hoped she'd understand. I slipped bites of vegetables under the table into the tote for Stuart and listened to him nibble and, once in a while, say something about Lance or someone else nearby into my mind.

Listening to my familiar while other people were around was going to take some practice. I kept glancing at the others whenever Stuart spoke, expecting them to have heard him. Which, of course, they hadn't because he was speaking in my mind.

Even telepathically, it sounded like he was talking with his mouth full. I'd have to wait for another time to fully wrap my mind around that nugget.

"Rory?"

I raised my eyebrows at Cam. "What?" It was obvious by his expression I'd missed some question he'd asked me. I was so sleepy.

He grinned and rubbed my shoulder. "I asked if you wanted me to take you home. You look asleep sitting up. I don't think you should drive your truck."

"Oh. Yeah. That sounds good. I'm exhausted."

"Oh, come on!" Lance said, holding up his wine glass. "Have a drink with us. The night is young."

I gave an apologetic look to Isla and said, "I'm so sorry. Almost any other evening, I'd be up for it, but this has been a long, hard day."

"Someone was murdered at a 5K run that Rory hosted this morning," Isla explained.

"Murdered? Woah. That's heavy. Do they know who did it?"

Suddenly, I wasn't so sleepy. Something about Lance's energy . . . his tone . . . had shifted.

In the tote, Stuart stopped munching the lettuce I'd pulled out of my salad and tossed him, becoming very still. *Careful. Something's strange here.*

Yeah. I felt it too. "No," I said carefully. "It's under investigation."

"You're investigating?" Lance met my gaze, his as pleasant as usual, but there was something under it. What was it?

"No," I lied. "Of course not. I'm an event planner, not a detective." I got to my feet and pulled the tote up with me. "Casey Norton, the sheriff, will investigate, along with the rest of the police department. Or, I mean, whoever she assigns to do it. Which isn't me. I mean, why would it be?"

Stop, Aurora.

I clamped my mouth shut, swallowing the nervous jumble of words trying to spill out.

"Oh, of course." Lance smiled again, flashing white teeth. "How silly of me. Must be the wine." He hefted the glass again, turning toward Isla.

My best friend pressed her lips together for a second. She met my eyes, and I tried to use telepathy to let her know I didn't want her to tell Lance I was, indeed, investigating the case. But, of course, I could only talk to Stuart that way.

But actually, that wasn't quite right. Isla and I were best friends. Had been for decades. If there was anyone I could communicate with without words, it was her.

She cut her eyes back to Lance and smiled. "Rory's a lightweight. She's a bear once she gets tired too. We should probably let her go before the claws come out." She winked.

Cam rose and took my elbow. "I'll get her home and tucked safely in her den. Tomorrow, she'll be sweet as a cub again." He kissed my temple.

"Thanks. I'm sorry I wasn't more social tonight, but I had fun anyway." I gave a miniscule jerk of my chin at Isla.

"I'm going to walk them out. Be right back." She jumped up and followed us away from the table. I could feel Lance's eyes on us.

"Don't tell him I'm investigating, please," I whispered.

"I got that. Why not?"

"I don't know. I think I should keep it under wraps as much as possible." That wasn't the reason. I'd told Roger, after all, and he was a suspect.

When we got to the door, Cam said he'd pull up with his car. I turned and gave Isla a tight hug. "You going to be okay with him? Do you want to make an excuse to leave with us now?" I asked in her ear.

She pulled back and studied my face, a frown on hers. "Why?"

"I have a slightly uneasy feeling about him." I glanced back at Lance to find him still watching closely. "He gives me the creeps or something."

Isla's frown deepened, then she shook her head. "I think I'll be okay. I have my Taser in my purse."

I barked out a laugh. "Where'd you get that?"

"Online. A single girl needs to be ready for anything. Go home and get some rest. Don't worry about me." She squeezed me one last time and headed back toward Lance, who smiled broadly at her.

The strange feeling I'd had at the table had evaporated. He gave off the vibes of a regular guy on a date again.

Cam pulled up, and I headed toward the car, feeling better. Isla could take care of herself. Even if the Taser didn't work, she knew some martial arts and was plain street smart.

I got in the car, the tote with Stuart in it on my lap, and fell asleep almost before Cam pulled away from the curb.

Chapter 8

"There was a draft into my cage last night." Stuart sounded even more disgruntled than usual.

I slumped over the kitchen table, chin in my hand. "You're not supposed to be on the table."

He sat straighter. "Why?"

"Because it isn't sanitary. We eat on this table, and you walk on those huge feet." I yawned and grabbed the coffee mug that said I Woke Up This Dazzling and took a careful sip. "Now we're going to have to disinfect."

"I'm perfectly clean. And you're ignoring my complaint about the draft. I don't want to sleep in the cage—tonight, I'll stay in your bed with you."

"The northwest corner is the best spot, but she's difficult to get out of it." Sasha's voice came from the living room.

I scowled in her direction, then leveled the same look at Stuart. "You can't sleep in bed with me. You're too small and fragile. I don't want to hurt you."

Sasha called helpfully, "She is very unwieldy while sleeping."

"I am not... I sleep normally! It isn't my fault if you get hit in the eye when I turn over. I'm asleep. And my bed is small. There's only room for me." I lowered my voice. "Stuart, I'll put your cage in a different spot. We'll find somewhere not drafty, okay?"

He heaved a sigh big enough for a full-grown man. "I suppose. But I want a pillow too. You can put one in for me."

"Fine." I added stopping at the department store for a new pillow for Stuart onto the mental to-do list I had going for the day. After I'd drank half the coffee in my mug, I got up and made some toast. I slathered it with peanut butter, refilled my mug, and leaned against the counter. Around a bite, I said, "I'm heading out first thing this morning. I have a lot to do."

"I don't like that tote. You'll have to find something else for me to accompany you in."

I kept chewing, mainly to hold in the snark that wanted to erupt in response to all his demands. After I'd carefully counted to twenty-five chews and swallowed, I said carefully, "What's wrong with the tote?"

"The bottom isn't flat. My feet get crunched together, and I can't keep my balance with all your moving around. It's like you're dancing or something. Do you dance while carrying me in the tote?"

"I don't dance." I gritted my teeth, then parted them to stuff the toast in my mouth again. I chewed furiously, taking out my irritation on the innocent food item.

"I need something with a flat bottom, or I feel out of balance."

The toast was gone. It was all on me to keep my patience now. "I'm not sure I have anything flat. But you can stay here if you want. I'm just going to be doing my thing. You know, asking people questions and all that. Nothing exciting."

"I wouldn't say you don't do anything worth being there for," Stuart said, finally hopping off the table onto a chair. "That man at the restaurant last night had a weird feeling to him. I think he's dangerous."

"What man?" Sasha was in the living room doorway.

"Lance. He showed up in town and wants to date Isla now. She made me and Cam go on a double date with them last night."

Sasha looked thoughtful. "This is the man who first asked Isla to move away from Shady Corners?"

"That's him." I wiped crumbs off my shirt and pushed away from the counter. "I was shocked to see him here. And he gives me weird vibes too, but I can't put my finger on why. But I'm not going to see him right now anyway, so there's no need to worry," I finished with a bright tone.

The familiars didn't seem to care about my optimism.

"I don't like it," Sasha said. "Stuart and I should both stay with you today."

I choked on my coffee. Two super annoying magical beings tagging along criticizing me all day? *No, thanks.*

When I was able to breathe normally again, I shook my head. "I don't think that's necessary."

"You can't fit in the tote with me," Stuart said to Sasha with derision. "I don't actually fit in the tote with myself."

"You fit! Be still, and don't pitch your weight one way or another suddenly, and you'll be fine."

"I don't need to be in the tote. I'll go along my regular way. You can keep the tote to yourself." Sasha lifted a paw and licked it delicately.

I shook my head. "No. Please do not go your regular way and show up out of nowhere to scare the bejeebers out of me. I hate that."

Stuart made an adorable rabbit snuffle and turned to show off the heart on his face. "I still want something other than the tote to ride in. I think she should buy me a soft-sided carrier. That way, I'll be balanced right—they have squared bottoms."

"I'm not buying... why are you talking as though I'm not here? I'm here! And I deserve to have a say in what animal tags along while I'm doing things and how they travel."

They both leveled me with flat stares.

It only took a moment for me to squirm under their intense gazes. I threw up a hand. "Fine! I'll get you a new ride. And Sasha, I have no control over what you do or where you show up to freak me the heck out. So, whatever."

"Why are you yelling, honey?" Mom swept into the kitchen already dressed and with her makeup on.

"Sorry, I didn't mean to yell. These familiars are driving me crazy."

"Aw." Mom scooped up Sasha and kissed her forehead. She was rewarded with a gentle purr. "They're so helpful, though. You should give them a chance."

I grumbled a little but gave in. I actually did have firsthand knowledge that Sasha could be quite helpful in a crisis. She'd helped me figure out what to do in a sticky situation more than once.

"We're training this morning, right?" Mom set Sasha gently on the floor and went to the cupboard to get her a tin of canned cat food. Sasha purred even harder.

"I need to talk to some people today, and I wanted to get an early start."

She didn't look happy with that answer but pressed her lips together for a second. I could see she was holding back her opinion, which I was positive had something to do with missing training the day before and possibly today. After a moment, she said, "Who do you need to talk to?"

"Linda Pearson for one, but I can't figure out a great way to approach it. She lost her husband—I feel bad showing up and asking a bunch of uncomfortable questions." *Been there, done that, felt bad about it.*

"Oh, I bet I can help."

"You can?"

"Let's go to the market, shall we? I suspect, if we hang around there long enough, we'll see Linda." Mom stirred creamer into her coffee.

"The town farmer's market? Why do you think she'll be there?"

Her lips turned upward. "I know Linda Pearson from the church ladies' group, back before I left town. She's incredibly detail-oriented and concerned about presenting the best when she hosts a get-together." Her smile became full-blown. "She has a funeral luncheon to plan for, and I'm quite certain she'll want to choose each piece of produce and every flower stem for it herself."

"Huh. That's a good thought, but why do you think she'll be there this morning? I'm sure she has a lot of other stuff to do today, too, what with losing her husband yesterday."

Mom waved away the concern. "The market is close to the funeral home. If we miss her at one, we'll see her at the other. She'll need to pick out a casket and music for the ceremony."

I was willing to give it a shot. "I still don't see how you know she'll be doing those errands today. Couldn't she do them tomorrow?"

Mom shook her head. "Linda will want to get everything done as soon as possible. In case she runs into a snag and needs extra time to find the perfect butter for the luncheon or something. She's a little ...type A." She polished an apple on her shirt. "Trust me."

"Sounds good to me. But you don't need to come. I saw Linda at the 5K, so I'll recognize her."

"You may recognize her, but she won't give you the time of day, I promise. She may even pretend not to hear you talking and walk right past. But she won't ignore me."

"Why?"

"Because we were in ladies' group together. She'll consider us peers and won't dare refuse to talk to me. She'll be too afraid of that getting back to the others."

"Wow. There are a lot of etiquette rules I'm not aware of going on here."

She winked and tossed the apple core in the trash. "That's why it's good you have my help. Consider me your sidekick for the morning."

I chuckled and got to my feet. "I'm not sure Casey Norton will pay you, but I'll share my crappy per diem."

"Not necessary. I'll just be glad to be together." Her eyes brightened. "Oh! We could train on the way."

I shook my head, amused. "Sure, Mom. We can do that. Let's go. Come on, Stuart."

I held the door open while Stuart ambled out and then Mom. Sasha didn't follow immediately, so I shut the door and made for the truck.

I stopped short. "No truck." Cam drove me home last night because I was too tired to drive. I turned back toward the house. "Stuart, either you ride in the tote for now or you hop for a while because I have to walk to the truck."

"Fine. I'll go in the tote," Stuart grumped.

"Great." I went inside, grabbed the bag off the hook I'd left it on the night before, and dropped it on the walkway.

Stuart jumped in and hunkered down.

I picked up the bag with an oof and walked next to Mom.

By the time we got to my old red truck, I was sweating, despite the fact that it was only in the mid-fifties. Who would have thought carrying a little ole bunny would increase my exertion so much?

I hefted him onto the passenger seat, surprised he didn't have any snide comments about me needing to do more cardio. A peek into the tote explained why—he was fast asleep.

Did rabbits sleep eighteen hours or whatever a day like cats?

I had no idea and knew I was woefully unprepared to own a bunny.

Manuals. I needed to get to them.

With a sigh, I shoved him to the center spot so Mom could sit in the passenger seat. Maybe he'd remain asleep while we talked to Linda. One could hope.

Firing up the truck, I glanced at Stuart to see if the noise would disturb him. He made a slight snuffling sound—was that a snore? It was the most adorable thing ever—and kept his eyes closed.

Mom ran me through some magic drills as we drove, until I almost lost control of the truck because my concentration wasn't on the road. "We're going to have to do this later."

"I suppose." She pointed. "Pull over there. We can see both the farmer's market and the funeral home from the lot."

I did as directed, shut off the car, and checked Stuart. Still sleeping.

Mom watched me. "You know, Sasha had a big hand in your familiar assignment."

"Did she?" That was news to me. "What does that mean?"

Mom reached in and stroked Stuart, and his whiskers twitched, but he didn't wake up. "Sasha got to know you and your habits over the past few months. She wanted to make sure you didn't get a familiar who wouldn't be compatible with you."

Okay, that hit me in the feels. "Wow." I looked at the rabbit. "He's kind of grumpy, though."

She chuckled. "I've never met a familiar who didn't have a bit of an attitude like that toward humans."

"Aren't they humans too?"

"They were once. Hundreds of years ago. But they're pretty far removed from that now. Our modern mannerisms and stuff sort of mystify them. They're almost like aliens, trying to get by in a foreign landscape."

I frowned, thinking about that. It hit home. I needed to be more patient. "That was nice of Sasha."

Mom gave a tight-lipped grin. "She talks a gruff game, but she's devoted to our family."

"Okay, I get it. I'll buy Stuart a more comfortable bag and carry him around without complaint." I hesitated. "With less complaining, anyway."

With one last smile, she reached for the door handle. "There's Linda. Perusing the lettuce, like I expected her to be."

I jerked my neck around to see where Mom was looking. Sure enough, there was Linda Pearson, bundled up against the cool morning air and sifting through the produce with a disapproving frown.

Mom jumped out and strode toward Linda. I scurried after her, much less gracefully, grabbing Stuart's tote at the last second. He didn't say anything, but I felt him move around inside, trying to get into a balanced position, most likely. I focused on carrying the bag as straight as possible to make it easier for him. What Mom had said struck home. Stuart was my familiar, which was weird because I'd never expected that to happen when I went in the animal shelter. So, I could give myself some slack for being disgruntled in the beginning. But I needed to start trying to make things go smoother between us.

"Linda, I'm so sorry." Mom got to the widow right before I did and reached out her hands.

Linda dropped the lettuce and took them, squeezing. "Thank you."

"Are you shopping for the funeral luncheon?" Mom gestured toward the produce.

"Yes, but I'm not happy with the selection today." Linda had aristocratic features, with high cheekbones, a pointy chin, and brows tweezed to within an inch of their life. The corners of her mouth dove down naturally, and now, she pushed them down farther. "I don't know what I'll do."

"I may be able to help." I stepped forward.

Mom beamed. "This is my daughter, Rory."

"Yes. You ran the event that killed my husband." She didn't take my proffered hand.

I dropped it, self-conscious, and rubbed it on my pants instead. "I'm so sorry. I want you to know I'm helping with the investigation. We're going to figure out what happened and bring your husband's killer to justice."

Linda pressed her lips together, giving the frown even more definition. "Why are you helping? Not making enough with your little business?" Her eyes darted toward my mom, and she softened her tone. "I mean, did you need to take on a second job to supplement yourself?"

Huh. Mom was right. Linda *did* care about what the church ladies might think of her, and she wasn't going to outright insult me in front of my mother. "Casey asked me to help."

"She deputized Rory," Mom put in, pride in her voice. "Rory has helped the department in the past, and the sheriff noticed."

"I see." Linda turned back toward the lettuce, picked up a head, and dropped it again with a disgusted twist of her mouth.

The woman had a very expressive mouth, I had to give her that. "Mrs. Pearson." I kept my tone gentle. "I'm sorry for the indelicate question, but do you have any idea who may have wanted your husband dead?"

She shot me a glare, then glanced at Mom again and puffed out a breath. "They already arrested someone, so I'm not sure why this is necessary. But everyone wanted to kill my husband."

I blinked. That was not the answer I'd expected. "Everyone?"

"Probably not people who never met him before, but most people who met him immediately wanted him dead, yes. And it was that mathematical thing. You know the one? Where one variable rises equally with another. What's that called?" She snapped her fingers as though trying to summon the word to her like it was a dog.

"I can't remember." I felt pretty lost. Definitely like I had no control of the trajectory of this conversation.

She shook her head and shifted over to look at radishes. "The longer people knew Strom or the more they were involved with his business dealings, the more they wanted him dead."

"Ah." I got it then. "You mean like the folks who rented from him?"

"Yes, like the animal woman who shot the projectiles that killed him."

This conversation wasn't going in the straight line she'd mentioned before. Whatever it was called. I made a mental note to ask Dad. He was good with math. "So, you think Candace killed him?"

She glanced at me and managed to squeeze a whole heap of judgement into the ten-second eye contact. "I suppose. She shot the weapon, he died, the police arrested her. I don't understand why you're here."

I shook my head. "Just doing my job. Did you know Candace very well?"

"I knew her as well as I knew any of Strom's lessees. I saw her a few times at the animal place when I tagged along on his rounds." She shot a look at the radishes that would wither them if they weren't already kind of wilty.

"Did you go with him often?"

"Not often enough," she shot, with venom that took me by surprise.

Lines appeared on Mom's forehead. "Linda, what's wrong?"

She huffed out a breath, turned toward us, and hissed in a whisper, "Strom was cheating on me." She straightened, looked around, and then said, only slightly louder, "I was considering killing him myself soon. Or maybe her. I hadn't decided yet when someone else offed him for me." She lifted her chin, as though defying us to take her to task for her murderous intent.

Mom's jaw dropped. It was the first time I'd seen her speechless since I wore jeans, a halter top, combat boots, and turquoise hair to senior prom.

Linda spun around and headed for the tomatoes, Mom and I trailing her like puppies.

Completely shocked, confused, totally bewildered puppies.

"Um, who was your husband having an affair with?" Mom asked gently.

Linda whirled around, surprised to see us still there. Then she crossed her arms. For a second, I thought she'd tell us to go sail a boat, but then she spat out, "Janelle. His realtor."

Mom winced. "You caught them?"

"No. But my PI was closing in. I know I'm right. He was with her all the time, not buying properties at the rate he was hanging out with her. If she knows what's good for her, she'll slink away and never show her face to me again. Now, if you'll excuse me, I have funeral food that isn't going to plan itself." She marched away, heading for the attendant. She looked mad as a wet hamster.

A man intercepted her. I recognized him from the 5K as one of the people who'd pulled Linda off Strom. I whispered that fact to Mom.

"Linda, honey! You look upset. What's going on? How can I help?"

Linda deflated a little. "Oh, Axel. I'm glad you're here." Distress edged her tone. "There's no good produce. How can I serve this horrible stuff to the mourners?" She looked about to cry.

I frowned. How had she gone from furious to infantile in two point four seven seconds? She wasn't as upset about her husband's murder as not being able to find decent peppers.

"It's okay. We'll figure this out. There has to be another supply of produce available." Axel looked around and spotted us. "Oh. You're the event planner lady."

"Rory." I gave an awkward half-wave and then forced my hand down. "How are you?"

"I'm...devastated at the loss of my best friend. Trying to help his wife cope. In the market for some decent produce. Any ideas?"

"Actually, no. But I could call my friend, Isla. She's a caterer. She may have a lead on some good stuff."

"That would be amazing. Thank you." Axel put an arm around Linda and leaned close to murmur to her.

I glanced at Mom. Her lips pursed as she watched the two.

I knew what she was thinking. They seemed kind of lovey-dovey. Was Linda having an affair too? With Strom's best friend? If Linda hadn't already given us a motive for killing her husband, this would hand us one on a silver platter. Getting a spouse out of the way to make room for your own affair without losing spousal benefits was a time-honored motive for murder.

Axel handed me a card. "Please call and let me know what your friend comes up with. We're willing to pay top dollar for half-decent kale."

Linda sagged deeper into Axel's side.

"Will do," I promised, sticking the card in my purse.

Mom grabbed my arm. "We'll leave you to it. My condolences, Linda." Without waiting for an answer, she pulled me toward the truck. "Wow," she mouthed as we went, looking over her shoulder at Linda, Axel, and the cowering produce guy. When we were in the truck, she said, "I can't believe Strom was cheating on Linda."

"She said she hadn't caught them. But she and Strom's best friend were canoodling pretty closely too."

Stuart said, "That woman is a main suspect if I ever saw one."

"The bunny's right," I said. "She's moved up considerably on my list."

Mom appeared thoughtful. "Do you think we should talk to the PI? He could tell us what evidence he had found so far."

I shook my head. "Let's skip the middleman."

"What do you mean?"

I grinned at her and started the truck. "I'm going to find Janelle."

Chapter 9

I tried to talk Mom into letting me drop her off, but she insisted on going with me to see Janelle. She said, "You might need me, honey. These types of matters of the heart are best dealt with delicately."

"I'm delicate!"

She gave me an indulgent mom-smile. "You're lovely, sweetheart. A dear girl. But you're sort of a bull in a China shop sometimes. We can't have that in this sort of situation. But it's okay. I can help."

"First, I'm not a bull. I don't know where you got that. Second, I doubt Casey would like me taking someone else along to talk to people about the case."

"What people don't know rarely hurts them."

I snorted. "I don't know about that. Seems like Strom didn't know his wife was onto his affair, and that certainly could have hurt him. At least, it might've made him not be on guard."

"She wants you to be done with this case so you can train." Stuart spoke aloud, so Mom could hear.

She sent him a glare. "Hey. I was on your side. Didn't you hear me make your case to Rory a little while ago? Why are you turning on me?"

Before Stuart could answer and start a whole back-and-forth thing that would slow me down, I said, "Mom, it's been more than two months since you came back. Since we went to Alaska, and I had a big leap in my magic-using abilities. We haven't seen any sign of Xavier." I remembered how, in February, she and Sasha had felt what they called Xavier's eye pass our way. I didn't understand what they had felt, and nothing had come of it. "He could have given up." I didn't want to say they may have overreacted in the first place.

She gave me a narrow-eyed look that said she heard my unvoiced thought. *Moms.* "He didn't give up. I know him, Rory." She turned to gaze out the window. "He won't give up."

"Okay. The thing is I'm much better with magic than I was a couple of months ago. If he comes, I'll take care of it."

"Mmm."

What did that mean?

How did moms manage to be so maddeningly cryptic? Did they take a class while they were pregnant or something? Before Lamaze and after Diapering 101?

I didn't feel like arguing about her coming with me anymore, so we traveled the rest of the way to the real estate agency a search of Janelle Realtor on my phone pointed me toward in silence. I'd turned my mind toward the upcoming discussion with Janelle, but I was willing to bet Mom was stewing about Xavier and my lack of commitment to training for a fight with him.

My right shoulder was starting to get tender, so I put Stuart's tote on my left, but it was awkward there. So, when I went through the building's doorway, I bumped him into the frame. *Ouch!*

"Sorry," I whispered.

This wouldn't have happened with a nice, thick, soft-sided carrier, he grumbled.

I thought about my vow to try and get along with him better. *I'll get you one later today. I promise.*

There was no one in the lobby, so Mom and I stood around awkwardly for a few minutes. I spotted a dish full of jellybeans on the receptionist's desk next to a porcelain Easter chick, and I couldn't resist grabbing a small handful. Then I wandered down a hallway, looking into offices and popping candy in my mouth, until I found a woman. I quickly realized she was the second person at the fun run who had helped Linda off Strom. This must be Janelle.

She was on the phone and held up an index finger to me. I backed away fast, not wanting to seem like I was eavesdropping.

Retreating to the lobby, I set Stuart on the floor to rest my shoulder. He grumbled some but settled down fast.

Mom still didn't appear to be speaking to me.

The woman appeared a few moments later, smiling brightly. "I'm sorry for the wait. We've been tremendously busy this season, so I'm the only realtor here, and our receptionist called in sick this morning. What can I help you with—selling or buying?"

"Oh, neither. We wanted to talk to you about... er..." I stammered to a halt. Should I tell her I was working with the police department or not?

Mom smiled graciously. "Is Janelle here?"

She waved a hand up and down her sides. "In the flesh. Did someone refer you to me? Because I like to send a thank you gift when my clients show their support in that way." She looked over her reading glasses at Mom, then me.

"No. We have a delicate question for you. Are you sure there's no one else here?"

Janelle's expression became guarded right away. Her eyes dance between us again. "This is about Strom." It was a statement. She focused on me. "You were there yesterday."

"I was. I'm an event planner, and the Run or Dye was my event. Casey Norton asked me to fill in for her, asking questions of those who knew Strom, and we talked to someone who suggested we speak with you."

"Me? I don't see what I can add. I don't know anything about what happened."

"We've been told you may have been close with Strom," Mom said. "What was your relationship with him like?"

She blinked a couple of times, leaning her head to see over the rims better. "Relationship? He was my client. That's all." Her eyes darted away, not making contact with mine or Mom's.

Interesting. She was hiding something.

Some rustling came from the back of the building.

Calmly, Mom said, "It sounds like one of your co-workers has returned. Maybe we should go to your office to continue."

"Yes. Fine. Come with me. But I can't talk for long—I'm busy." She glanced over her shoulder. "Why are you helping the sheriff, again?"

"Oh, to give her a hand," I said, wincing at how awkward that was.

Mom rolled her eyes at me. "The sheriff has found herself in need of hiring more staff. Until she can do so, she's brought

Rory on as a temporary deputy because she already had a background and fingerprint check on file."

Okay. Not true, totally, but far less lame than what I'd said.

We went into Janelle's office, which was small, but she'd decorated it in a way to make it look bigger, with minimal clutter and an almost completely cleared off desk.

She sat behind it, and we sat across from her. I put the tote on my lap.

"I'm going to cut right to the meat and potatoes course here, Janelle," I said. "Were you having an affair with Strom?"

She stiffened. "Of course not. Did someone tell you that?"

"I can't divulge who, but someone made an accusation, yes."

"Whoever it was didn't know what they were talking about. I have a boyfriend." As soon as the words were out of her mouth, she winced.

I was pretty sure she also blanched a little, but the room wasn't well-lit.

"Who's your boyfriend?" Mom asked.

"This is ridiculous. Why do I have to tell you things about my personal life that have nothing to do with Strom?" She started to rise.

"Tell us about what does have to do with Strom, then," I suggested. "Did you help him buy any rental properties?"

She dropped back to her chair, and her jaw clenched before she answered. "Yes. A few. He worked with a different realtor before me, so I'd only been around long enough to help him with a couple before...well, before yesterday."

A middle-aged man with brown hair appeared in the doorway. "Janelle, there's someone up front for you. It's one of your clients. I would have asked her to wait for you, but she's worked up about something. I thought you'd want to know right away."

She shot to her feet and almost ran to the doorway. I wondered whether she was that eager to get away from us or that keen to calm down an upset client. Probably the former. I'd want to get away from us too—we were asking some uncomfortable questions.

Janelle edged past the man, brushing shoulders with him. "Thanks, Troy. I'll be right back."

Troy hung around in the doorway, looking unsure whether to leave us or not. He decided against it and came in, perching on the edge of the desk nearest to me. "You'll be happy using Janelle as your agent. She's a real go-getter."

"Oh, yeah? That's good to know," I said with a smile. Mom shot me a look, and I gave a tiny shrug I hoped she would see and Troy wouldn't.

"Yeah, yeah. She's real good. Of course, now that Strom Pearson is gone, the rest of us may be able to make some deals on development properties. They had the market cornered on it for a while."

"Development properties? You mean like empty places to build on?" I leaned forward, but Stuart squirmed in the tote as I squished him, and I jumped backward again to give him more room.

Troy kicked his leg back and forth, thumping the desk repeatedly. "Yep. Pearson got a bee in his bonnet over the last six months or so that he wanted to become a developer instead of a landlord, I guess. Or both, I don't know. Janelle was his realtor on it, and they were killing it. Strom had gathered up a whole handful of properties. The rest of us didn't have a chance with those two sharks in the water." He chuckled like he'd made a hilarious joke. Then he waved a hand. "Nah, I'm joshing you. I don't have any interest in trying to deal with development properties. Too much red tape. I can barely get my regular real estate deals done without messing something up." He pressed his teeth together and drew his lips back. "Oops, I guess I probably shouldn't be saying stuff like that out loud. What I meant to say was I love being a real estate agent, so please send your friends and family to me if they want to buy or sell a house." His laugh was thin and annoying. "But, since you're talking to Janelle right now, I guess you'll probably send people to her." He got to his feet awkwardly. "You'll be okay here until Janelle comes back." He said it is a statement not a question, and then he hightailed it out of the room fast.

"Development?" Mom said.

I was already on my feet, having transferred the tote to her lap. Keeping one eye on the door, I went around the desk and opened the top drawer on the righthand side. I figured that was the one most people used for things they needed multiple times a day. Unless they were left-handed. Then, they might use the top left drawer. But Janelle must not be left-handed because her planner sat in the drawer on the right side. *Bingo!* I pulled it out and paged through to the current week as fast as I could, then used a finger to scan the lines.

She had met with Strom several times and almost every day the week before. The meetings were at her office, at his office, and at coffee shops. They all said the same thing: *Meet Strom to discuss deals.* And then, on each entry, were jotted notes about various properties. Some said things like *too small* or *not enough parking* while others said *perfect for an apartment building* or *could make a great retail spot.*

I slammed the book shut, returned it to its drawer, and slid it shut.

By the time Janelle returned a few minutes later, I was studying a framed picture on the wall. Over my shoulder, I said, "Your client okay?"

"She's fine." Janelle's tone was short. "Why are you two still here? I told you I wasn't having an affair with Strom. I have a boyfriend."

I motioned for Mom to get to her feet. "Yes, I think we've covered everything we wanted to for this visit. We may come back with more questions after we got further along in the investigation. We appreciate your cooperation."

Janelle blinked rapidly a few times, as though in disbelief that we were not going to question her more.

I took the tote from Mom, and we headed for the door. "Bye, now."

She didn't answer.

When we were back in the truck, I let Mom in on what I had seen in the planner. She pursed her lips and looked out the window, thoughtful.

I was deep in thought, too, so I didn't mind the quiet. I couldn't help but believe Janelle was hiding something. But what was it? The most obvious thing would be that she *was* having an affair with Strom. But was that it?

Who else could I talk to who could corroborate one way or the other?

A gasp from my mother, coinciding with Stuart popping his head out of the tote, drew me back to the present.

"What's wrong?" Then I felt something. A creepy feeling, like bugs scampered across my skin. I fought the urge to bat at them, focusing on the road. I pulled the truck safely onto the shoulder, threw it into park, and unbuckled. I shoved my sleeve up, but there was nothing there. Still, my skin crawled.

Mom grabbed my hand over Stuart, who cowered between us as though a coyote had marked him for the day's lunch. "It's Xavier," she breathed.

"Where?" I swiveled, trying to see out of all the truck windows at once.

She shook her head. "Not his physical presence. He must be scrying."

"Scrying?" I knew the word essentially meant magically searching for someone's location, but that was about it. "Wait, is this what you and Sasha have felt in the past?"

She nodded, and I noted she'd blanched considerably. Even though she'd said Xavier wasn't physically near, her eyes darted around outside the truck too. "Yes. He hasn't looked here for a good while, but he definitely is now."

"Why can I feel it now too?"

"It's all your training. You've opened yourself up to more of the energy webs around us. Stuart and I feel it differently than you—we can't access the webs the same way you can as a spirit witch. I feel it as a pressure on my magic, like someone's trying to remove it from me." She shuddered. "He's focusing here. Not looking away."

"What should I do?"

She shook her head. "I don't know," she whispered. "There may be nothing you can do."

We sat together, gripping hands, until the weird feeling subsided. Mom drew a deep breath, as though someone sitting on her chest had finally moved. I rubbed the skin of both arms, trying to forget the cringey feeling. Then I started the truck and headed into town without a word.

Chapter 10

I parked outside my office and sat for a moment. Silence filled the cab of the truck. Finally, I said, "We'll figure out what to do, Mom. Don't worry."

She smiled, but it was easy to see the dread in her eyes. Until she'd told me about Xavier, I'd never seen that in my mother's face before.

I didn't like it.

I pulled my phone out and dialed Isla. When she answered after two rings, I blew out a relieved breath. I hadn't realized I'd been worried about her in the back of my mind. Even though I knew she was able to take care of herself fine, I'd been uncomfortable leaving her with Lance the night before. "You okay?"

"Sure, but you sound weird. What's up?"

I glanced at Mom and decided to hold off telling Isla about Xavier. I'd wait until we were alone—my mother was totally freaked out. I didn't want to upset her more.

Instead, I said, "Do you have a lead on some super-fine produce? Mrs. Pearson didn't like the farmer's market offerings for Strom's funeral luncheon. I told her I'd check with you."

"Super-fine is my middle name. Not because of produce, though."

"You should go into stand-up. Produce?"

She snort-laughed. "Yeah, I can get some Grade-A stuff for her. I need to know how much and what. My supplier can probably deliver this afternoon or tomorrow, as long as the buyer's good for the money."

I said, "I think Mrs. Pearson can afford it. I'll get a list of what they want and call you back. Thanks, hot stuff."

"That's super-fine to you."

I ended the call with a chuckle and then dug out Axel's business card and dialed. He answered with a question in his tone. "Hello?"

"Hi, Axel. This is Rory Aspen—from Aspen Events? We spoke at the farmer's market."

"Oh, hey there! Did you track down some lettuce for us?"

"Sounds like I can get whatever Mrs. Pearson would like for her luncheon. I need a list and a guarantee to pay, and it can be delivered today or tomorrow."

"Fantastic! How about you come to my office? I'll get with Linda and have the list ready if you come in, say, fifteen minutes?" He gave me the address, and we hung up.

I checked my map app and found that Axel's office was only a few minutes away. "Mom, do you want me to drop you off at home?"

She shifted her eyes to look at me. "I think I'd better stay with you."

A frown snuck onto my face. "You're worried about Xavier?"

She nodded.

"Okay. You can stay with me. Listen, I was thinking. Is there a way for us to scry for him? Like he was scrying for me? If we can determine exactly where\he is, we could try to head him off at the pass." I peeked in the carrier to check on Stuart. He was awake but with half-lidded eyes, as though about to fall asleep.

"I'm not skilled at scrying. Your grandmother was."

"Dad's mom?"

"Yep."

I'd found my grandmother's journal around Christmastime. Mom said the reason I was a spirit witch may have to do with the fact that I had witch genes from both sides of the family. They'd skipped my father, but he knew about magic.

"I wonder if she had any books or anything that could teach us how."

I can teach you.

With a little jump, I twisted to look at Stuart again. *You scared me.*

You'll need to get used to this. It's the best way for us to communicate.

I understand. I'm sure I will. But you did it for the first time yesterday, so...

Stuart huffed and said out loud, "I know how to scry. Sasha does too."

Mom was interested. "We should go home and do it right now." Her expression morphed to puzzlement. "I wonder why Sasha never thought of this before."

"It's forbidden," Stuart said, then yawned.

"Forbidden?" I yelped. "By whom?"

Stuart didn't answer, so Mom took up the explanation. "There's a council. Or two. I can never remember exactly how it works, but there's a governing body of some sort for witches."

"I see. And they don't like scrying?"

Stuart said, "It's considered too easily misused to disrupt someone's privacy."

"Okay, I can actually see that. But Xavier's doing it, huh?"

"Xavier's an evil wizard." His tone added the *duh* that he didn't say.

"Right. And we're not, so we shouldn't break the rules." I gave Mom a hopeful look. "Should we?"

She bit her lower lip and glanced at Stuart.

He stared back with his big, brown eyes and floppy ears, for all the world looking like a regular, adorable, non-magical bunny. Then he sneezed.

"Bless you," Mom and I said together. Then we giggled, and the heavy feeling that had been in the car since we'd felt the creepy eye of Xavier lifted a touch.

"I think we should scry," Stuart said. "I know it's forbidden, but this is an emergency."

"Is there, like, a permit we can apply for or something?" I asked. "Maybe if we told the council how mean Xavier is, they'll understand we need to know his location?"

Stuart blinked at me. "No. There's no permit. We simply decide to break the rules and hope we don't get caught."

"What happens if we get caught?"

He lifted a shoulder in a passable imitation of a shrug. "We all lose our magic, and the familiars lose their bodies."

Chapter 11

I followed the map app to Axel's office, which was in the basement of a building loaded with suites that all looked alike. The top half of the building was mostly doctor's offices while the lower was a mish-mash of accountants, lawyers, and other professionals. We passed a cluster of offices sharing a lobby that included an acupuncturist, a talk therapist, and a massage therapist.

"Ah, a one-stop-shop," Mom commented. "Not the best atmosphere, though." She referred to the chipping paint on the walls and dusty furniture.

I agreed but didn't say anything. I shifted my tote to the other shoulder. A backpack may work better for carrying Stuart around. That way, I could spread the weight over my upper back and not have it all hanging off one shoulder or the other.

I decided to surf the web for some cute backpacks when I had time. One of those kinds for babies. That made me chuckle. The next thing you knew, I'd be purchasing a stroller to push him around in or something. I could already imagine all the looks I'd get.

What was my life becoming?

Axel's office was in the bottom corner of the building, but it was surprisingly bright and nice inside. I wondered why he didn't upgrade to something above ground.

A receptionist greeted us warmly, setting her reading glasses on the desk blotter. "Mr. Price is waiting for you. Come on in." She led us through a door into Axel's office. He was on the phone behind a mahogany desk. He smiled and held up a finger. We sat and waited for him to finish and hang up.

"No, no. It's fine. I'll handle it. Okay. Talk to you later." He hung up and turned his thousand-watt smile on us. "Thanks for coming. I can't tell you how much this helps. I didn't see what was wrong with the stuff at the market this morning, but Linda has exquisite taste. And I think planning the luncheon down to the tiniest of details helps her feel a sense of control right now." A frown pulled his lips down. "It's got to be so rough to lose your husband suddenly like that. Right before the vacation of a lifetime too."

"They were going on vacation?" I transferred the tote off my lap to the floor by my feet. Stuart exuded so much body heat that I needed space from him.

Axel looked sad. "They were taking a cruise to Greece. It was all Linda wanted to do for the past twenty years, but Strom kept putting her off. He was a workaholic. Plus, with all those properties to care for, there was always something coming up. He could have hired a property manager a long time ago, but he liked to oversee everything himself. I guess I was the closest thing he had to a manager."

That didn't jive. According to anyone I'd talked to about Strom's landlord abilities, he didn't have any. At least, he never took care of or paid for any problems that came up with the properties. What Axel said didn't make sense. Strom wasn't spending all his time caring for his rentals.

"It's too bad they never got to go on the trip," Mom said, wistfulness in her voice.

I jerked my eyes to her face. Was she playing a part, or was she thinking about her own life with Dad? I thought back on their marriage. They hadn't gone on a lot of trips. Actually, none with only the two of them. I'd always been with them, and it was stuff parents take their kids to do—Disney, the Grand Canyon, that type of thing. Was Mom pining for a romantic cruise to Europe with Dad?

I made a mental note to talk to my father about this later. If he knew Mom wanted to do something like that, I had no doubt he'd make it happen for her.

And maybe I should start considering moving out. Letting them have some space. It had been good for me to be there with Dad while Mom was gone, but she was back now. They had time to recover.

I dragged my attention back to the conversation. Axel was speaking. "—I urged her to still go. Of course, it will be bittersweet without her husband, but she'll need to keep living now that he's gone. She can make her own memories. Restart her life, so to speak. And she can find someone to go with her."

Hmm. Did Axel want to be the one to go with Linda? Had he killed Strom for the opportunity? I tried to think of a way to dig deeper into that angle. To find out if Axel and Linda were having an affair.

"It seems like you're there for Linda right now," Mom said, giving Axel a sympathetic look.

Man, she's good. I'd have to consider sharing my measly earnings from the police department with her after all.

Axel ran a hand over his hair. "Strom was my best friend." His voice broke, and he rubbed his nose and mouth as his throat worked. A moment later, he resumed with a clear voice. "I'll do what I can to care for and help his widow. That's all I can do for him now."

"Had the two of you been friends for a long time?" I asked.

"Since college. We met at State. I actually moved here after school because he told me how nice it was. Said there were a lot of opportunities, too, even though it's a small town. And he was right." He gestured around the room. "I've done pretty well in the insurance game here. Plus, I was near Strom. It was nice having a buddy to play golf or barbecue with or whatever over the years. I didn't grow up having close buddies, so it was nice." He choked up again and looked at his hands. "Sorry, this is all so new for me. It's hard to believe he's gone."

"Sorry for prying."

He shook his head. "It's okay. I want to talk about him. I'm going to miss him so much."

"You know, Strom didn't have a great reputation around town," Mom said, her tone gentle. "Was it hard being his friend?"

He widened his eyes. "No, not at all. I mean, I know some people didn't like him, but that was the authority thing, you know?"

"Authority thing?" I asked. "What do you mean?"

"People don't like paying for things, right? Monthly bills. They start hating the ones they owe the money to. It wasn't

Strom's fault. It was the position of authority he held over them."

Authority, huh? I'd never thought about landlords that way before.

"Who do you think killed Strom?" Mom leaned forward.

He stared at her. I thought he wouldn't answer. But then he blew out a breath. "Candace from the animal shelter. I guess she was particularly resentful of having to pay Strom every month. She shot him with metal instead of dye." He put his face in his hands, and his shoulders shook.

Mom exchanged a glance with me and then jumped up and went around the desk to give Axel a half-hug around the shoulders. "I'm sorry for your loss."

He wiped his face with a sleeve. "Look at me blubbering. I think I'll be a wreck at the funeral. Oh, but you don't want to sit here and watch a full-grown man fall apart, do you?" He grabbed a sheet of paper from a pile and handed it over the desk. "Here's the produce Linda wants. Thanks again for getting that handled for us. It's such a load off her shoulders, and that makes me happy. It would have made Strom happy."

I stuck the list in my tote.

Hey, watch it! You'll paper cut my eyeballs!

Sorry.

It was easy to forget I had a familiar in my bag when he wasn't weighing down my shoulder like a thousand-pound rock.

I got to my feet. "Call if there's any other way I can help you or Linda."

"Thanks. I'm sure we have everything else covered, but I'll keep it in mind."

We headed for the door, but I turned back. "Do you know anything about Strom buying development properties?"

A line appeared between his brows. "Development?" He shook his head. "No, he never said anything about that to me. Why?"

"I heard it through the rumor mill," I said. "Have a good day."

I felt his eyes on my back as I walked through the reception area.

Chapter 12

I stuffed three fries in my mouth and felt simultaneously joyful and guilty. They were so greasy and exactly the right amount of salty. I knew I was eating for comfort, which was where the guilt came from, but I shoved away the thought. I reminded myself there was such a thing as comfort food for a reason, and it was okay to enjoy it sometimes without beating myself up.

Across from me, Mom took a big bite of brownie and closed her eyes.

Her comfort foods were sweet, and mine were salty. We made quite the miserable pair.

"Okay," I said around the bite. "Let's go over what we know. Strom was killed by metal projectiles in the dye gun. Candace was the one who procured the canisters, but Roger loaded the one that killed Strom."

"And both of those people had motive to kill him because he was a jerk of a landlord to them," Mom responded, readying another bite on her fork.

"I'd say Candace was the more desperate of the two. She was worried about losing the animal shelter completely. Roger was okay, but he for sure didn't like the rent hikes."

Mom took a sip of water. She set the fork down. "I should save the rest for later."

I picked up two more fries and waved them in the air. "These won't warm up well. I have to finish them now."

She grinned. "Okay, the next suspect is Linda."

"Yeah, she mentioned having considered killing him. Was she joking?"

"I don't think Linda jokes," Mom said. "Though if she had killed him, you'd think she wouldn't have said that particular thing to us."

"Right. But maybe she's just that angry."

Mom picked up her fork and loaded it with a piece of brownie. She popped it in her mouth and widened her eyes when I shot her a look. "A tiny bit more is all. I'll save the rest."

"Not on my account." I stuffed more fries in my mouth and said around them, "Linda thought Strom was having the affair with Janelle."

"Janelle did seem to be hiding something when we talked to her."

"I got the same feeling." I frowned at my empty plate. "I should order another round."

"They don't have alcohol here, dear."

I gave her the side-eye. "I meant another round of grease." I pushed the plate away with a snort and leaned back, resting my hands on my belly. "Nah. I'm good. You know, I think I know what to do next. I'll drop you off at home, okay?"

"What? But honey, I thought we were going to scry for Xavier. We should do that right away."

I held up a hand. "We will, I promise. I have one thing to do first. And you shouldn't go with me because I'm not going to be exactly following Casey's instructions on this next bit. I mean, not to the letter anyway."

Mom gave me the look. The dreaded one that involves one eyebrow arching and infinite depths of pressure on that one area of a person's soul that a mom knows how to manipulate perfectly. I squirmed. "I don't want you to get into trouble, that's all. I'll let you know what I found as soon as I'm done, okay?"

"Aurora, you haven't been following the letter of Casey's law all day. I don't think she would want you taking me anywhere while you are investigating. But you did. Besides, I don't care that much if she gets angry with me. And what's she going to do, not give you the measly amount of money she promised? Fire you?" She shook her head. "I stay with you today. After what we felt in the truck, I stay with you."

I glanced into the tote at my feet, expecting to find Stuart asleep, but he stared up at me and twitched his nose.

I threw up my hands. "Fine. You can come with me."

She leaned back and looked smug. "Good. Where are we going?"

"To the police department."

"WHY ARE YOU HERE?" Casey leaned against the door jamb of her office and glared. "Didn't I say you should only come here if I called you?"

"Yes, but I need to see the evidence." I twirled a wrist over my head. "And that's in this building somewhere, right?"

"It is. And you don't have access to it." She pointed at Mom. "She for sure doesn't have access. Why are *you* here?"

Mom gave an ingratiating smile. "Casey, dear. I haven't had a chance to talk with you about this promotion of yours yet. I know it was thrust on you, but you're doing a great job. All the ladies at my book club think so too. I mean, three murders in four months! Can you imagine? I doubt our old sheriff would have been able to make heads or tails of it, but you're doing a stunning job."

"Oh. Thanks."

Casey's expression reminded me of a puppy baffled at being pushed off a couch, not understanding he wasn't a person and furniture was off-limits.

"You're welcome, dear. Now, this latest murder is quite baffling, isn't it? I mean, Strom Pearson was a pillar of the Shady Corners community." Somehow, Mom managed to inch forward and get Casey to back up to allow us entry into her office.

It was tiny and dingy, like the rest of the police station. This town needed to invest in fixing up this building. Mom wandered around, looking at pictures on the wall that were left over from the previous sheriff. She frowned. "You should get your own things in here."

She was right. It was depressing.

"Soon," Casey said. "I suppose. And as for Pearson, he wasn't exactly the pillar you named him. He was an almost universally hated figure. A terrible landlord with a near monopoly on rental properties for businesses."

"That's what we've found out too." I picked up a paperweight from the desk and hefted it from hand to hand. It was in the shape of a trout. "Do you fish?"

She shook her head, lips thin.

Ah. Not hers. I was getting the idea that Casey hadn't redecorated the office because she still felt like an imposter in the sheriff position. It was sad.

"What else have you found out? Or is this your first stop?" Casey took the paperweight and set it back on the desk, then perched in front of it, so I couldn't handle anything else.

"I've talked to lots of people!" I told her about Candace, Roger, Linda, Janelle, and Axel.

She blinked a few times. "That actually is a lot of people. What are your thoughts?"

"Lots of different motives. But I keep thinking about the dye gun itself. And the cartridge Roger loaded into it—the one filled with metal that killed Strom. If Roger's telling the truth and he simply grabbed a canister from a box, then who put it there?"

"Candace is the obvious choice."

"Let me look at the canisters."

"No."

"Why?"

"Because you're not actually law enforcement. And if you mess something up, they won't be admissible as evidence." She met my gaze, defiant. "Didn't you read the manual?"

I skated past that question, hoping she didn't notice. "I won't mess anything up. You can even stand there and watch me if you want."

Mom said, "I'll wait in the truck. One less person for you to worry about." Her smile was sweet as fresh peach pie.

Casey looked between us, then made a grr noise. "Fine. I'll show you, Aspen, but only for a minute. And you have to glove up."

I winked at Mom. "No problem."

Mom split from us in the hall, heading to the front of the building while Casey and I entered a stairwell. I followed her down two flights, the air getting damper as we went. "This building needs a dehumidifier. Or a stronger air conditioner or something. If this is how it feels in the spring, it must be ridiculously humid in the summer."

Casey didn't answer. So much for bonding over small talk.

She led me down a dreary hallway with flaking green paint, unlocked a concrete door, and waved for me to enter the evidence room.

There was only one table, loaded with stuff, in the center of the room and a few metal chairs, one with only three legs. "There's only evidence for one crime in here right now?" I knew Shady Corners didn't have a lot of crime, but this seemed strange.

"Most evidence gets sent to the city when the trial moves," she explained, kicking a foot up onto the wall and leaning back. "Hurry up. I have somewhere to be in fifteen minutes."

I fought the urge to glare at the sheriff and grabbed gloves out of a box on the table. As I slipped them on, I looked over the bagged items, which included several dye guns. Once my hands were covered, I pulled out the bag with purple dye splotches on it and verified it was the finish line gun by peering at the label. I turned it over in my hands. "I've never used one of these."

"It's basically as easy as pointing and pulling the trigger. You load the canister in the back. It clicks in. Pretty easy."

I set the gun down and moved to the canisters. They were long and filled with a few dozen balls. My eyebrows pulled together. "There are multiple paint balls in each canister?"

"Yeah. They're not the same as paint balls, though—they're designed differently, so they don't hurt, but they open easier."

"Okay, but there are a lot in each canister. So, if you exchanged one to have something else in it, how would you guarantee it was shot out at the right time?" I flipped the canister around and held it up for her to look.

She pushed off the wall and came over. After putting gloves on herself, she opened the bag with the murder weapon and released its canister. She held it up. "It's empty."

"But Roger filled it with a new one right before it was shot at Strom. There should still be lots of balls in there."

She gave me a deadpan expression and continued to hold up the empty canister.

"So, there was only one ball in the canister...that means someone knew Strom was about to cross the finish line and put in a canister containing only the fatal ball."

"Logical." Casey returned the canister to the gun and rewrapped it. "Seems to me, if Roger confessed to loading the gun, then he's our most likely suspect, not Candace. He must have lied about putting in a full paint canister."

I couldn't argue with her. But it didn't sit right.

"I'll get a warrant for his arrest."

"Wait. Do you have to do that right away? Can't I do a little more digging first?"

She regarded me with such a blank expression that I couldn't get any read at all on what her answer may be. Finally, she gave me a jerky nod. "Okay. I'll give you a few hours, but no more. If you don't have something that can convince me otherwise by dinner time, I'm getting the warrant." She yanked off her gloves and headed for the door.

I followed, slower, mind reeling. How was I going to get this done? Talk to Roger again? No, what else was he going to tell me? I'd have to attack it from the other direction. Find more compelling evidence that someone *else* had killed Strom.

Or not. In which case, Roger would be arrested, and Mira would probably never forgive me.

Chapter 13

We went home to regroup and eat. Stuart munched on lettuce, and Sasha came out of some hidey-hole, stretched as though she didn't have a care in the world, and blinked at us.

Mom slumped into a dining room chair and looked around. "Your dad must have taken Piper out for a run."

I grabbed two glasses from the cupboard. "That's good. It'll give us a chance to do our scrying without interruption."

"Scrying?" Sasha's tone was alarmed. "Who's going to be scrying?"

"We are." I set the glasses on the table and went to the fridge for iced tea. "We decided to try and pin down Xavier's location."

"Did you feel his eye earlier?" Mom leaned forward, eager for Sasha's answer, which the cat familiar didn't give right away.

Finally, she huffed, "Yes. But I still don't understand this scrying plan. We've felt Xavier's eye before. Scrying isn't legal."

"It may not be legal, but if the only other thing I can do is wait around for him to show up—and watch my mom be upset and worried all the time—then I'm going to give it a try." I held up a hand, cutting off Sasha's reply. "I understand it's not al-lowed. And I don't expect any of you to risk yourselves by helping." I wrinkled my nose. "But if you could at least point me in the right direction on how to do it?"

Silence fell for a few minutes. I used the time to pour tea for Mom and me, retrieve the sugar dish for her, and sit and sip mine unsweetened. While they considered the question of scrying for a wizard, I thought about how to track down Strom's killer before Roger got carted off to jail.

Who had opportunity to exchange the dye cartridge for one with shrapnel in it? And why hadn't Roger noticed there was only one ball in the new canister? He'd said he was a paint ball player, so that should have been something that jumped out at him.

Perhaps I *did* need to talk to Roger again.

And what about Janelle? She'd sworn she wasn't having an affair with Strom, but the two of them had been working on buying up development properties. Could something have happened between them that made her want him dead?

That gave me an idea, and I pulled out my cell phone, hitting the browser icon.

"I'm going to help Rory," Mom said quietly. "I don't know a ton about scrying, but, Sasha, if you'll give me a little guidance, I should be able to manage."

"You're risking your own magic, Elaina," the cat said.

"I know."

Sasha lowered her head, then brought it back up in a good imitation of a human nod. "I'll help you."

"You only have to give us some information, not be here when we do it," I said.

"I will help you," she repeated. "Elaina is my witch, and since she's decided this is necessary, it's my duty to be of as much service as possible to her while she does it."

"Me too," Stuart piped up around a bite of lettuce. "I stand by Aurora."

If that didn't give me a warm, fuzzy feeling, nothing would. "What do we need?"

We spent the next half hour discussing how to successfully scry for Xavier. The familiars listed off ingredients and told us we'd need to do the ceremony in the moonlight. When they were finished, Mom held up the list. "I'll get to work gathering all this stuff. I'll have to go to the herbalist's shop for some of it."

"Oh, can you pick some of that amazing blueberry tea she has while you're there?" I asked. "I love that stuff for an afternoon cuppa. It's got a good jolt of caffeine and tastes amazing."

"I'll get some." Her tone was full-on indulgent mother.

"Thanks. In the meantime, I have an errand to run. I'll be back by dark, so we can set up. Is Dad going to be okay with us doing this?"

Mom considered that. "I think so. Your father has never argued with me about anything having to do with magic. He knows it's not his wheelhouse and lets me take the lead."

"Maybe it's best not to tell him we could get into trouble for it?"

She leveled a stern gaze at me. "You mean not tell your father the whole story? Is that a tactic you employ on a regular basis with your parents, Aurora Aspen?"

"What? No. Mom! We're talking about a very specific thing here, not my life in general." She had such a knack at making me feel thirteen instead of thirty.

"I see. Hopefully your father and I taught you that a lie of omission is still a lie." She hadn't dropped the mother tone.

I ducked my head. "Yes, ma'am." Sliding out of the chair, I grabbed my phone. "I'll be back." I hurried out before Stuart could demand to tag along.

THE ANIMAL RESCUE BUILDING was locked and dark, as I'd hoped it would be. I hadn't been sure, since it was only late afternoon, but I'd taken a gamble that Candace would be between feedings.

I scooted around the side and let myself into the gate at the back. The yard was empty—all the dogs were tucked away inside. I crept to the back door, hoping there were no motion-detecting lights or anything else that would pop on and alert someone to my presence while also blinding me. Luckily, nothing happened.

The back door was tightly locked, but it was nothing a quick pull on the energy webs around me and a bit of intention couldn't handle. The doorknob lock clicked, followed by two louder deadbolts sliding open. A memory of the first time I'd picked a lock with magic danced through my mind. I'd needed Sasha to coach me through that. It was pretty amazing how far I'd come.

I held my breath as I opened the door, waiting to hear alarm klaxons go off. But my gamble proved to be a good one.

Strom had been too miserly to pay for a security system. I slipped inside and closed the door.

Dim emergency lights shone at intervals in the hallways. Afternoon light shone in the rooms I passed, further illuminating the way.

I hurried to the supply closet I'd seen Candace get rabbit supplies out of while I was there. It was too dark to see much inside, so I pulled out the mini-flashlight I'd stuffed in my pocket and turned it on.

After five minutes of rummaging through bags of cat litter, extra food bowls, and hamster bedding, I closed the closet door and moved to the next room.

When I got to the dog runs, a few of the occupants barked at me. I hurried over to reach through the bars and give ear skritches, which settled everyone down, so I was able to continue my search through the closet in that room after a few minutes.

In the cat room, the occupants couldn't care less that I was there and ignored me roundly. As I'd expected.

I checked all the closets I could find in the building but found nothing related to the paint guns or canisters.

My search ended in the lobby, and I stood by the counter thinking about what to do next.

I should get out of here before I get caught—that's what I should do next.

I scanned the room one last time and turned to head for the back door again. My arm brushed a stack of mail on the counter, and envelopes floated everywhere. With a groan, I crouched to collect them. Most of it was junk mail, but one envelope caught my attention—the return address had Janelle's name on top.

I returned the rest of the mail to the counter and regarded the envelope closer. It was addressed to Candace, not the shelter. What was a realtor sending a letter to a renter for?

I flipped it over and frowned at the seal, wishing it were open. I stood there, indecisive. I could do a spell to pop the seal easily enough, read the letter, put it back, and reseal it. But should I? Tampering with mail was a federal crime.

"Heh. Like breaking and entering isn't," I muttered.

I held up the envelope and shined the flashlight at it. There was no way to read the letter, but I could see something nestled inside. A check. I squinted, trying to make out the amount, but it was impossible.

What had Janelle paid Candace for?

A dog yipped in the kennel and several more joined in. I slapped the envelope on the pile and streaked for the back door. I didn't slow down when I got outside but darted around the building, through the parking lot where Candace's car now sat empty—how had I avoided her?—and down the street a block to where I'd left my truck. I jumped in and sat still, trying to get my pounding heart to slow to a normal rate.

When I finally felt stable again, I started the truck, did a U-turn, and headed away, wondering why Janelle had sent Candace money and how I was going to find out.

THAT NIGHT AFTER DINNER and after I was successful at begging Candace on the phone to give me more time before she arrested Roger, swearing to her that I was close while I crossed my fingers behind my back, Dad took Piper out for her last walk. Mom and I hurriedly set up the coffee table for scrying in the living room. We followed Sasha and Stuart's instructions and used the herbs Mom got earlier in the day to make a circle with the table at its center. Mom pulled a necklace off over her head and handed it to me.

"This is pretty." I held it up to examine the sphere-shaped crystal hanging from a black cord. "I've never seen you wear it before."

"I picked it up from the herbalist's shop. Stuart said a nice clear crystal would help with the scrying."

"Wow. I guess it's lucky they had one."

"Wrap about six inches around your hand." Stuart perched his front paws on the table, shaking his head when one ear fell over an eye. It fell right back in. "Keep six inches hanging still."

I followed the bunny's orders, though I'd never been great at estimating measurements. When I thought I had it about right, I held it up with a question on my face.

"Good enough," Stuart said. "Now, we'll need moonlight to stream over the table."

"Got it." Mom jumped up and drew back a curtain until light fell across me.

"What now?" I adjusted my position. "My knees are going to hate me tomorrow."

"Now we crush the herbs together and sprinkle them around the map."

Mom grabbed the already waiting mortar and pestle and went to work while I straightened the map of Shady Corners. It didn't help—the thing was as wrinkled as an elephant from being stuffed in my glove compartment for at least a year. I ended up having to fetch four books to hold the corners down.

When the herbs were sprinkled per Stuart's specifications, we looked at him expectantly. He said, "Now we all meditate, concentrating on Xavier's whereabouts." He dropped back to his haunches next to Sasha. "You hold the crystal over the map with a loose wrist. Don't even think about the fact that you're holding it, Aurora. Focus on your meditation. Don't worry about paying attention to its movements at all." He looked around at each of us. "No one should break meditation until the crystal hits the map. Oh! Elaina, do you have the personal item of Xavier's?"

She pulled a pair of cufflinks from her pocket. At my raised eyebrows, she shrugged. "He left them at my house after a dance once when we were dating. I found them in the bottom of my jewelry box."

"Set them on the edge of the table, right in the moonbeam," Stuart directed. Then he sneezed.

So cute.

I must have given him too much of an adoring look because he glared and said, "Time to get to work."

Everyone settled in to meditate. I plopped down on my rear end and crossed my legs, hoping it would be more comfortable than leaning on my knees.

My lower back immediately objected to the plan, but I ignored it and focused on meditating.

Silence filled the house but for our soft breathing and the ticking of the grandmother clock in the corner of the room. It was soothing and helped me focus even faster.

Once I was calm and breathing regularly, I allowed the idea of Xavier to coalesce in my mind. I focused on it completely. Though I didn't know what he looked like, my mind helpfully created an image for me to study. It was a laughable conglomeration of every cartoon wizard or sorcerer I'd ever seen on TV. He was gaunt, with dark circles under flashing black eyes, greasy raven hair that fell to his shoulders, a hooked nose, and a sapphire blue robe. My concentration wavered when I almost burst out laughing.

Managing to fight down the mirth and recover my focus, I studied the wizard in my mind's eye carefully. When he looked me in the eyes, I directed a sharp thought his way. "Where are you?"

His already beady eyes got narrower and more evil as they seemed to attempt to send laser beams into my skull. I held his horrible gaze without flinching, focusing on keeping my breathing and heart rate calm and steady. Dimly, I heard the sound of the kitchen door opening and Piper's padded paws prancing across the floor, but I refused to drop the meditation. It felt like we were close.

A sharp pain jabbed the back of my arm, and I almost lost concentration.

Seriously, I needed to get back to yoga with Isla if I couldn't even hold up a necklace for a few minutes without my tricep cramping up. I put it out of my mind, shoving the discomfort away until it was only a dim, ignored thought like all the others I'd released in exchange for focusing on Xavier.

The training I'd done with my mom and Sasha was paying off. I'd never been able to focus this well during mediation pri-

or to the many sessions I'd had with them over the past couple of months.

Xavier blinked. His form in my mind shimmered, and shock coursed over his features.

The crystal plunked onto the table.

My eyes popped open to find my mom's wide ones staring back at me. Sasha and Stuart climbed onto the table with their front feet, and we all focused on the map.

The crystal's point was directly on a specific address. I drew in a breath that threatened to choke instead of oxygenate me. "Oh, no. That's Isla's house."

Chapter 14

"What is that?" Dad stood over the table.

Mom reached for him, and he pulled her to her feet. I could've used the same treatment—my back and hips felt locked in place. *Seriously, Rory. Stretching and exercise program, stat!*

"We scried for Xavier," Mom explained. "And he's here." She looked stricken.

"At Isla's house." My heart thudded along, faster and harder than usual. "It's Lance. I knew something was weird about him. I should have insisted Isla send him away."

I tore for the door, ignoring the pins and needles in my feet. At least they weren't asleep enough to send me crashing to the floor. Score one for not being *completely* out of shape.

"Aurora!"

Skidding to a halt, I shot a look at Stuart. "What?"

"I'm coming with you." He hopped toward me faster than I'd ever seen him move but still slowly. I scooped him up, stuffed him in the tote, and struggled to slip on my shoes. The inanimate objects seemed to resist all attempts to smash them onto my feet.

"I'm coming too," Mom said.

"So am I."

We both stopped and looked at Dad. "Um. I don't think..." I started.

Mom put a hand on his arm. "You should stay here."

Frustration coursed over his face. "I'm not useless simply because I'm not a witch." He pushed past me, stooping to get his tennis shoes on. "I'm coming. This Xavier has terrorized my family long enough. It ends tonight."

I glanced at Mom. She chewed her lip. Dad had that tone. The one he rarely used, but when he did, it meant there was absolutely no way he was going to back down. I figured he used to use it on his patients when he was done entertaining ideas about alternative treatments he knew wouldn't work.

Piper whined and nudged my hand. "You too?" I puffed out some air. "Fine. We'll all go. But only because I don't have time to argue with any of you." Every moment Xavier slash Lance was alone with Isla was time he could use to hurt her.

As I jogged to the truck with Stuart's tote on my shoulder and Piper's leash in my hand, I berated myself for letting Isla get into this predicament. If she got hurt, I'd never, ever forgive myself. It would be all my fault. For being a witch—a special spirit witch not seen in centuries—and having her as my best friend. Being in my orbit meant being at risk from Xavier. Why hadn't I left Shady Corners when Mom and Sasha said I should? I'd been too stubborn, insisting I wouldn't run away from my life.

At what cost?

Moments later, we were squished into the cab of my truck like crayons in a box, and I squealed out of the driveway. I could barely form coherent thoughts as we careened toward Isla's house. I should have taken a second to text her before we left.

No, I couldn't spare that second. Like I couldn't waste time arguing with people—and animals—who wanted to come along.

My parents talked in low tones next to me, but my brain refused to decipher what they were saying. I could only think of my best friend, alone in her house with a raving mad dark wizard.

What had I done?

"SLOW DOWN, HONEY. GETTING pulled over isn't going to help Isla."

Dad's tone was gentle, and even though I wanted to argue, I bit my tongue because he was right. There weren't too many cops in Shady Corners, but it would be my luck to run into one of them and get waylaid for fifteen minutes when I needed to be at my friend's house.

I pressed the brake, slowing down to exactly the speed limit.

"Isn't that Janelle?"

I followed Mom's finger, craning my neck to see around my parents. Sure enough, the realtor headed into a building. "Yeah, it is."

Mom frowned. "That's Axel's building, remember?"

She was right. I wondered what business the two of them had with each other. "She could be going to some other office. Like that one-stop-shop."

She chuckled. "Somehow, I didn't peg Janelle as the type to spend a lot of time getting therapy. Plus, it's late. I bet she's going to see Axel."

It was possible. And I'd love to stop, sneak in, and verify it. But there was no way I was going to take the time. I'd have to figure it out later.

I pulled up next to the curb across from Isla's house and down half a block. We all peered toward her place. "Someone's there," I breathed. An unfamiliar car sat on the curb in front of the Victorian, and light spilled from the back corner, where I knew the kitchen was. "I'm going in."

"Me too." Dad hopped out before I could argue.

I groaned, and Mom patted my hand. "I'll look out for him. You focus on Xavier. We'll all help as much as we can, but I have a feeling most of this is going to be up to you, honey."

That was how I wanted it. "No problem. I'm ready to get rid of this maniac. And if he so much as *insulted* Isla, he's going to be sorry." I surged out of the cab before she could answer, rage causing a physical burning sensation in my gut. Or it could be fear.

It was going to be rage, I decided, because fear was weak, and I needed strength in the next few moments.

As I hurried across the street and approached the house, I took a moment to focus on all the energy webs around me. I drew in magic and held it, hoping to be able to release it quickly if needed. That wasn't something I'd worked on a lot in lessons yet—probably would have started if I hadn't been investigating Strom's murder.

Guilt crashed into me. I shoved it away. Feelings could be dealt with later. It was time for action, and I needed all my focus on what was going on.

I crept along the side of the house and peeked into a window. I felt Dad arrive beside me, and I held out a hand to stop him. Lance and Isla were in the kitchen, cooking together. Ivan sat on the counter supervising, flicking his tail back and forth. They must be making something he wanted.

Lance faced my way, and I jerked back, ramming my father's side with an elbow.

"Oof," he said.

"Sorry," I whispered. "Lance is in there, looking this direction. I don't want him to see me until I figure out what to do."

At least Isla had looked fine, laughing and sipping from a glass of wine. That could change at any moment if I confronted Lance, though. A thought occurred to me. I grabbed Dad's hand and ran back to the front of the house, reuniting with Mom, Piper, and Sasha on the sidewalk. "I want to get Isla away from Lance before I talk to him."

Mom said, "That's a good idea. Then he can't grab her as a hostage or something."

I winced at the thought, handed Stuart's tote to Dad, and pulled out my phone. I scrolled to Isla's number and paused, racking my brain. How to get her out of the kitchen?

My thumbs hovered over the screen for a moment as I considered. Then I had an idea, and they flew over the buttons. *Hey, super-fine, can I borrow that rose-colored, tea-length dress? The one with the small white roses on it?*

I hit send and then waited impatiently for an answer. It took several minutes, and I imagined her setting down her wine, pushing Ivan off her cell phone, and picking it up to read the text. At the exact moment I visualized her responding, the speech bubble came up to let me know she was about to. "Yes! She's answering," I whispered to the others.

The text came back: *Sure, but you're going to have to come pick it up. I'm otherwise engaged.*

I can be there in five. Going out with Cam tonight and don't want to wear something he's already seen.

He's probably seen it on me, genius.

No sweat—I'll fill it out better. Hey, what are you otherwise engaged with?

She didn't answer immediately, and I wondered if she'd set the phone down and was ignoring me, but the speech bubble came up and I felt relieved.

You only wish you could fill out a dress as well as me. And I'm cooking dinner with Lance. So, I'm going to have to invite you to leave after you pick up the dress. We want some alone time.

Mom peeked at the screen. "You two text like fifty-year-olds. Complete sentences and actually writing out words? What are you, gen Xers?"

I elbowed her away with a scowl and answered Isla: *Fine. Meet me at the door—be there in two.*

She didn't answer, and I could only hope she had run upstairs to grab the dress. I turned to my parents. "Here's what's going to happen. I'll try and get Isla out of there—Dad, you do what you can to keep her outside. Mom, you and the familiars come in with me but stay in the foyer. I'll head to the kitchen and confront Xavier. If I need help, I'll call for you, but otherwise, please stay back."

"Honey, I don't think that's a good idea. We should all be right there with you—Xavier is strong."

"I know that, Mom. But we're going to do this my way, or you're going to stay out here entirely. I don't have time to argue with you about this."

The light went on in Isla's foyer. "That's my cue. You guys stay out of sight until I get her out." I ran up the stairs before they could argue, praying they would do what I asked and step into the shadows before I opened the door. For extra security, I slipped in as fast as I could and shut the door behind me. "Oh, you got it already. That's the one. Thanks."

Isla held the dress in her hand, but she cocked her head and gave me a suspicious look. "What are you really doing here?"

My gaze went over her shoulder toward the kitchen, but Lance didn't come out. "What do you mean? I'm here to pick up the dress." I held out my hand. "Just like I said."

She shook her head and tucked the clothing under her arm. "I don't think so. You hate this dress. Why are you here?"

My eyes darted back to her face and then to the kitchen again. "I don't hate it. And I think it'll match my hair nicely. Come on, give it."

She cocked her jaw, considering, and then held the dress out at arm's length.

I wanted her to step toward me, so I could grab her wrist and haul her out the door, but it was clear she was on to me. Isla didn't move forward, and I'd have to move away from the door to get the dress from her. Shuffling came from the kitchen. I for the doorknob behind me. "You need to get out of here," I hissed. "Now. I'll explain later, but for this moment, trust me, okay?"

She studied me for the space of three breaths, and I thought she would argue, but suddenly, she dropped the arm holding up the dress and moved toward me. "We were getting ready to have beef and broccoli. Lance is probably in there burning it right now. What is going on?"

At least she was whispering. As soon as she was within my reach, I put an arm around her back, opened the door, and shoved her out. Dad was waiting on the front porch, and he grabbed her, bent his head close to hers, and pulled her toward the steps. At the same instant, Mom, Sasha, and Stuart darted in through the door, and I closed it before Isla could change her mind and come back in.

I was going to get in trouble for that one the next time I saw my best friend.

But I couldn't care about that now. All my senses stretched down the short hallway toward the kitchen, where I could still hear rustling. Then movement caught my eye in the doorway, and I stiffened. But Ivan stalked out, tail in the air as though he was affronted by something. Lance had probably refused to give him a morsel of food. Evil wizards will be evil.

I knelt and rubbed my fingers together, and Ivan ran to me, purring and butting his head into my shins. I bent close to his ear. "Go upstairs and hide."

He turned and streaked up the staircase as though he understood me. Sometimes, I almost wondered if he was a familiar too.

I straightened to my full height, glanced at Mom, and made a motion to remind her to stay put in the foyer. Then I headed forward to the kitchen. When I got to the doorway, I peeked around the jamb, hoping to catch Lance unawares.

But he stared right at me. A smile played on his lips. "I was wondering when you were going to show up."

And there it was. Proof that he was Xavier and had been waiting for me to catch him. I cleared my throat, which was suddenly dry. I should've had a big glass of water before embarking on this particular adventure. *You shouldn't do magic dehydrated, Rory.*

I shook off the ridiculous thought and focused. "Here I am."

He chuckled. "Isla warned me that if I was going to get involved with her, I'd be seeing a lot of you too. I can dig it. Best friends are best friends, after all, and you two have known each other since you were toddling around, I guess." He glanced over my shoulder toward the hallway. "She's upstairs getting the dress you want."

My forehead wrinkled. Was this guy for real? He thought I was there in the capacity of Isla's best friend rather than as the woman he'd stalked for years, so he could steal my magic and kill me? I blinked a few times, trying to figure out the best way to approach the situation. I drew a little more on my magic, getting ready to cast some kind of spell on Xavier, not that I knew exactly what I was going to try and cast at him yet.

Suddenly, I could see more white around his pupils, and I realized they had widened. He felt me draw the magic. He knew what I was doing.

"Let's drop the act, shall we? I know who you are. Let's end this right now."

His jaw worked as though he intended to say something, but no words came out.

I drew even more magic, thinking about what to do with it. "You've been following me for a while, trying to find me. Why didn't you attack me the last time you were in Shady Corners? When you pretended to be here trying to get Isla to move to Ann Arbor and work for you?"

His head shook a few degrees side to side. "I haven't been following you. Why would I attack you? I was here to try to get Isla to work for me, and I fell for her while I was at it."

Boy, did I want to zap him with a shock spell. Instead, I gritted my teeth and ground out, "Stop lying. The jig is up. We both know you're Xavier, so there's no more need to pretend."

His face scrunched in confusion. "Xavier? I don't know anybody named Xavier."

This time, I did send a bolt of magic toward him, along with my intention that it should cause a skin-crawling sensation to wind its way up his arms and legs.

He hopped around like someone had shaken his snow globe, rubbing frantically at his arms. "What did you do? Stop that."

The great, evil Xavier was weirded out completely by a little, tiny creepy skin spell? That didn't compute. "Who are you?"

"You know who I am! I'm Lance. Now stop tossing your magic at me."

I slowly withdrew the spell. "Okay, so you're going to try to convince me you're a simple restaurateur, but you know about magic? Please. Sell that to somebody a little dimmer than me.

Who are you?" I held up my finger menacingly, subtly threatening another skin crawly spell.

"I'm Lance," he insisted. Then he held his hands up, palms out. "Okay, okay. Isla wasn't the only reason I came up here the first time."

"No?" I said with mock surprise. "You don't say?"

Lance rolled his eyes and sank onto a barstool. "I'm not proud of it, but I needed the money."

"What money?"

"One day, this guy came into my restaurant. He said he was a wizard who'd had his power stolen from him. Part of his power, anyway. Stolen by a person whose name he didn't know, though he did know her mother. He said he thought he had narrowed down her whereabouts through scrying to Shady Corners, but he didn't want to come up here and snoop around himself because the mother would for sure root him out. He paid me to find the woman." His gaze met mine. "You."

My mind swirled around as I tried to decide whether to believe him. "So, Xavier came in and hired you to find me? How did you know who you were looking for? And why would you believe someone who said they were a wizard anyway?"

His spine straightened, and his chin came up a touch. "The type of magic my family has. We're great at seeing auras. The guy who hired me—you said Xavier, but he told me his name was Paul. Anyway, he told me what your aura should look like." He waved a hand to indicate the area around my body. "And it does."

I dropped my hand. "What does my aura look like?"

"Like the northern lights," he said matter-of-factly. "I've never met another person who had one that looked like that. Paul said that was how it would be. He was right."

"So, you found me and what? You went back and told this Paul all about me? My name, my business, my boyfriend, my best friend?" My voice rose as I got more and more upset. "You sold me and my friends and family out for a little money?"

He was shaking his head before I finish speaking. "No, it wasn't like that. Paul said he only wanted to get his magic back, that was all. And that seemed like fair play to me. I mean, stealing someone's magic is bad juju. Not cool." His tone was like that of a disappointed teacher. Like my disappointed high school math teacher, anyway.

I crossed my arms. "Don't you lecture me. I didn't steal anyone's magic. Xavier is trying to steal *my* magic. He's been looking for me for ages. And, Lance, do you know how he plans to steal the magic from me? The only way he *can* steal it from me?"

He tried to play it cool, but Lance's complexion blanched a couple of shades. "No, how?"

"By killing me. That's the only way he can take my magic. So, you've been duped, I'm afraid. Played right into his hands." A strange feeling skittered up and down my spine, and I whirled around, pulling on my magic. But there was no one in the doorway. I glanced over my shoulder at Lance, my eyes wide. "Where is he? That's why you came back up here, isn't it? Why it took two months after you found me for him to come. It wasn't enough for you to tell him who I was. Xavier wanted you to show him. Where is he?"

Lance's Adam's apple bobbed as he took a giant gulp. I could see in his face that he believed me—that he was beginning to realize what a huge mistake he'd made. He opened his mouth to say something, but a flash of lightning tore through the air outside, thunder following it almost immediately. Where there hadn't been even a drop of rain a moment before, a violent thunderstorm had erupted right over the house.

Chapter 15

"Get down!" I ordered, drawing more magic as I almost gave myself whiplash trying to see everywhere at once. Where would Xavier come from?

The lights went out.

Running footsteps thundered down the hallway, and my mother and the two familiars tore into the kitchen. "No! Get out of here," I ordered.

"He's here," Mom said with a shudder. "I'm not going anywhere."

"We are here with you, Aurora," Sasha said. "Come what may."

Another round of lightning and thunder erupted, and the front door opened. A moment later, it slammed shut, and I surged forward, creating a glowing ball to light my way as I went. I hurried down the hallway, wondering if I'd be confronting Xavier in the foyer in a moment, but it wasn't him. It was Dad, with Piper and Isla. "You guys! Get out of here. Go to the truck."

"What's happening, Rory?" Isla's tone was slightly scared but mostly irritated. Of course, I wouldn't have expected anything else from her.

"Xavier's here," I told her. "It isn't safe, and you all need to leave now. Get to the truck," I begged Dad. "Take Mom, Ivan, and the familiars with you." I hesitated and then, against my initial urge, added, "Take Lance too." Deep down, I didn't think he knew what he'd done.

Another lightning bolt. Another crash almost right on top of it. I gave Dad a gentle shove. "Go!" Relief rolled over me when he headed for the door. I spun around and made my way back to the kitchen, holding the magic ready.

I had no idea what I expected to see, but the man standing next to Isla's countertop when I entered the room wasn't it. The word that came to mind was *small*. He had a mop of curly brown hair and round glasses too narrow for his face. His clothes were throwbacks to the nineties, with a too-large green and black windbreaker over black polyester running pants with a green stripe down the leg.

He didn't look the same age as my mother—ten years younger or so, though I knew that wasn't the case.

When he saw me, he smiled, revealing a gap between his front teeth and crooked canines. "Finally."

Even though his voice sent a shiver of unease through me, I straightened and squared my shoulders. I touched the energy webs around me and basked in the warmth of the magic. There was something to be said for feeling big, inside and out. "Yeah, you're not very good at tailing people, huh? Ever heard of an internet search?" *Yeah, goad the evil wizard. That's one approach.*

His mouth twisted. "Your mother changed her last name. Such a ridiculous, antiquated custom. It's nice that fewer women are doing it now. Easier to track people down."

"This chit-chat is fun and all, but I had plans to freshen up my hair color tonight, so can we speed it up? You want my spirit witch abilities, right?"

Something behind Xavier's eyes lit up, like Piper's did when she smelled hamburgers grilling.

Oh, yeah. He was nuts.

"You can give it to me, you know. I have everything I need for the ceremony. If I don't have to break your will to transfer the power, you won't be harmed. Much." He tapped a complicated beat on the countertop with the fingers of his right hand. "If I have to do it the other way—take your abilities by force—I'm afraid you won't make it." His mock sad expression made me want to punch it off his face.

Wow, Rory. Didn't take long for this guy to inspire you to feel uber-violent.

The tapping fingertips got faster, and the thunder and lightning intensified. My eyes narrowed. "I'm not sure why you need my power. You seem to have plenty of cool abilities all your own."

His fingers stilled. "What, the storm? That's simply a parlor trick. I can only do it if there's already a weather system in the area. Mainly for show. Creating awe and all that." He moved away from the counter, a step closer to me, revealing Lance, looking uneasy, behind him. "No, I need the ability to tap into more energy webs to do what I really want. Right now, I can't even aim the lightning at anyone." His pout reminded me of a toddler whose mother handed him the wrong color sippy cup.

"You're not very nice, are you?" I fought the urge to move backward the same amount of space he'd come toward me. If

I'd learned anything from superhero movies, it was to always act confident, even when you felt all wobbly and Jello-y inside.

Xavier advanced again. "Nice or not nice. Who even cares? What's truly important in life is powerful or not powerful. And I'm going to be on the right side of that equation. Finally." He stopped five feet away from me. "Time's up. Are you going to give it over willingly, or am I going to take it? Live or die—it's up to you. See? Choices. I can be nice."

"Xavier!"

I groaned internally at my mom's voice behind me but didn't dare take my eyes off the wizard to turn and give her the glare she deserved.

His eyes fluttered wider. "Elaina." His voice was soft.

"Why are you doing this?"

He swallowed hard and spoke firmly. "I'm only taking what was stolen from me. You wouldn't want someone to get away with stealing from you, would you?"

"How did she steal from you? She was born with this gift, and you weren't. It's hers."

A flash of white fur behind Xavier caught my eye, and I almost groaned out loud. Did no one listen when I told them to flee the evil sorcerer? *Figures.*

He fisted his hands and snarled, "The power should have belonged to my child, where I could have benefitted from it. If you hadn't left me, it would have."

Mom crossed her arms and wrinkled her nose. "That's the most ridiculous logic I've ever heard. I could never have a child with you. You're way too selfish and moody."

Xavier's expression darkened.

Out of the corner of my mouth, I muttered, "Don't antagonize the wicked wizard, Mother." Not that I hadn't done the same thing moments before. I understood the impulse.

"Wicked? I'm not wicked. I'm someone who has been stomped on in all things, by all people. I'll have my due now, that's all." He raised his hands, and the air between us danced with visible sparkling static. "Decide. Now."

I lifted my hands too. The sparkles were a neat trick, so I made my own. Pink, to match my hair. "I did."

Fury overtook him, and he growled like a wildcat as he whipped his hands up and slashed them toward me.

In the blink of an eye, his staticky sparkles coalesced into a mini tornado and came at my head. I threw up a shield, so hastily I had no idea if it would hold. But the tornado bounced off the shimmering haze I'd created and dissipated.

Sweet! I was performing magic at the speed of thought—something Mom had been adamant I needed to be able to do to protect myself against Xavier. Even though I'd tried hard, over and over, it had never gone this well in training. Sasha had said I just needed more time for practice, but I'd had my doubts about ever achieving it.

Guess I needed a life-threatening situation to hone my abilities.

Xavier jabbed a flat palm toward me, like an overzealous air-high-five, and the shield I'd created caved, then burst with an audible pop.

No premature gloating. Got it.

Panic washed over me as I tried to think of what to do next. Xavier stepped closer and reached out one hand, which he slowly curled into a fist. My throat felt as though it was closing. I knew the wild fear in my gut must show in my eyes. What should I do?

His fingers twitched. My throat closed more. With his other hand, Xavier yanked a necklace off. An amulet, with a now-broken silver chain and tiny ruby gems studding the surface.

Wind brushed past my cheek as I calmed my breathing and took shallower, more measured breaths to conserve oxygen. Without my recent focus on meditation, I wouldn't have been able to pull that off through my terror.

The wind kicked up more, and I realized Mom was using magic, pelting Xavier with something that looked like hail. It irritated him as it struck his face over and over; he flinched and faltered, letting up on my throat a fraction.

In that instant, a horrible, eardrum-rattling sound rang out, and a white ball of fur launched itself onto the wizard's back.

Sasha.

She clawed, scratched, and bit, and Xavier dropped the magic aimed at me to swat at her. He screamed and staggered drunkenly around, bashing into the counter and then the table.

I rubbed my throat and drew in deeper breaths that felt like fire snaking down my windpipe. Mom advanced on Xavier, and for the first time, I realized my dad and Isla were there, too, in the hall outside the kitchen. I held up a hand to urge them back and turned toward the action, pulling on the energy webs around me for more power.

What could I do to stop Xavier?

The wizard gave a violent jerk, and Sasha flew off his back. My heart leapt as I watched her sail through the air, crash into the sliding glass door, and slump on the floor, unmoving.

"No!" Mom cried, rushing to her familiar and dropping her assault on Xavier. Isla slipped past me and knelt next to them.

Xavier, panting, straightened at the speed of a snail and pinned me with a horrifyingly furious look. Angry red slashes crossed his neck and ears where Sasha had gotten some claw swipes in. He wiped his mouth, gaze never leaving my face.

My mind went blank as I faced the hatred in his gaze. I had no idea what to do.

Aurora! It was Stuart. I didn't see him, but his voice was loud and clear in my mind. *Think of your strengths. Use them.*

My strengths? Now is not the time for riddles, rabbit. What are you talking about? Spell it out like I'm five.

Xavier, without taking his eyes off me, crouched and scooped up the fallen amulet. Then, quick as a snake, he darted forward and wrapped it around my wrist.

"No!" Stuart shouted, appearing from behind the trash can.

My eyes widened as I felt power seep out of me. I tried to hold onto it, to draw in more, but the faster I did, the faster it drained out. I glanced down. The rubies on the amulet glowed and pulsated.

It was happening. Xavier was taking my spirit magic abilities.

Weakness rolled over me in the form of a jolt of vertigo, and I sagged. I was so tired. I didn't care about the magic. Let him have it. I only wanted a nap.

Dad was there in an instant, keeping me from falling. He dropped Piper's leash, and she jumped and snapped at Xavier, frantic.

"No," I whispered. "Get Piper out."

Isla streaked across the kitchen, grabbed Piper's fallen leash, and pulled her away just as Xavier tried to backhand the dog, missing by an inch.

Anger fired in my belly, fighting its way through the malaise.

How dare he try and hit my dog?

But my body wasn't as furious as my mind. Not as strong. I sagged again, dropping hard to my knees. *Ouch. That'll hurt later.*

Later. If I couldn't get out of this, there wouldn't be a later for me. Sasha had made it clear the wizard taking my power like this would result in my death.

Xavier towered over me, holding my arm above my head with the chain wrapped around my wrist. He touched the amulet with his other hand, and the glow extended to his body. His spine stiffened as my power flowed into him like water into a balloon. He seemed to get larger, though I didn't know if that was real or a trick of my rapidly weakening mind.

Mom was back, pelting Xavier with magic, but it bounced off him like mosquitoes that hit a plume of repellant. She was saying something, but I couldn't understand it through the pounding in my ears. She should stop trying. It wasn't necessary. I didn't need magical ability. Let Xavier have it.

I leaned over, into Dad's arms, thinking about how nice it would be to go to sleep and have a nice rest.

No! Aurora! Your will!

Stuart's voice cut through the comfortable fog, jolting me. My eyes popped open. Xavier was breaking my will. It would kill me. I had to do something. It wasn't sleep trying to claim me, and I wasn't going to let death take me without some kind of fight.

I struggled to take in what was happening since I'd zoned out. Chaos had erupted in the kitchen. Mom sweated as she pushed spell after spell at Xavier. Isla swung a heavy iron pan, trying to clock the wizard in the head, but it wouldn't connect. He must have magically shielded himself from such a mundane form of attack after Sasha clawed him.

Speaking of Sasha, she was awake but lay panting, presumably too hurt to rise. Lance tried to help, chanting and holding his hands up as though he, too, was fighting Xavier with magic.

Stuart nudged my hand with his nose. *Look. He can't handle it.*

What was the cryptic bunny yammering on about now?

I followed his gaze when he turned his fluffy head to look at Xavier. Energy still flowed through the amulet to him, but something was wrong. He didn't look happy. His eyes bulged like a fish in open air. His mouth worked, but nothing came out. It looked to me like he was trying to back away, but the magic wouldn't let him. He was frozen, a vessel into which my power poured.

And he couldn't handle it? Perhaps the vessel wasn't big enough, or strong enough, for this type of power. Was Stuart right?

The spirit magic dislikes him. It's too good for him.

And then I knew what to do. I fought the remaining apathy off and gathered as much energy from the webs as I could, weak as I was. I imagined myself as a sponge and the magic as water droplets soaking into me. When I was maxed out and couldn't absorb another molecule, I took a breath, looked into Xavier's wild eyes, and shoved every bit of it through the amulet and into him.

The room stilled. Or maybe I only imagined it, but it felt like all the sound and movement was sucked out of the kitchen. There was only me and Xavier, staring at each other. The loss of my power felt like my very spirit had been torn from me. But I knew where it was. Waging a battle from inside the man before me.

And from the look in his eyes, I could see it would win.

Xavier's body jerked, his back bowing, and he seemed to vibrate at an impossible angle. A sound, resembling the word no but really only tortured wailing, erupted from him, and then he collapsed in a heap. Power surged back through the amulet, filling me with energy and joy.

Sound crashed back into the room. Everyone was exclaiming or asking a question or crying.

I twisted my neck to see Lance was the one crying, sagged against the door frame. He mumbled something over and over that I was pretty sure was, "I'm sorry."

Isla slid to her knees and grabbed my hands. "Are you..."

"I'm fine." I smiled, then put on my best robot voice. "Full power restored, Captain."

She squeezed my hands. "You pushed it to the last second, though, didn't you? Drama queen."

Mom knelt to feel the pulse in Xavier's neck. "He's alive."

"Yes, but powerless." Sasha was on her feet, thank goodness. "The magical ability he had on his own merits fled when yours left him, Aurora." She sat and eyed me. "Well done. His warped mind was no place for your pure, kind magic. It wouldn't stay with him."

"Hey. It wasn't all passive. I helped too." I got to my feet with Dad's help and pulled Isla up. She clutched my hand still, and I got the idea she wasn't planning on letting go soon.

"What do we do with him?" I gestured with my chin to the fallen wizard.

Mom grinned. "Put him on a bus to San Francisco," she said. "He always hated it there."

Chapter 16

I slept until ten the next morning, but when I woke up, I felt wonderful. For the first time in months, Xavier wasn't one of the first things on my mind. Well, he was, but I was thinking about how he'd never bother us again, not wondering where he was and when he'd show up to attack me.

Though I didn't actually know where he was. After about five minutes of feeling great after the battle, fatigue had hit me like the flu. Mom and Dad promised to take care of Xavier, and Isla had hustled me upstairs to her bed. I'd been asleep before she was out the door.

I looked over and found the other side of the bed rumpled. Isla must have slept there, but she was already up. Faintly, I could hear the sound of dishes clinking in the kitchen downstairs. I threw my legs over the side of the bed.

"You did well."

I jumped up, stumbled over a pile of clothes and spun around on one heel before my mind recognized Stuart's voice. He hopped out from under a pillow at the foot of the bed.

"Oh. Thanks."

He rubbed the heart-shaped mark on his face with a front paw. "Xavier won't be a threat to anyone anymore. When he woke up, he didn't remember you, your mother, or even magic."

"Wow. Why?"

Stuart did a weird jerky thing with his head and front leg that was his version of a shrug. "I don't know. It fascinated Sasha, though, so she'll likely ferret out the answer over the next few weeks or months."

"Did Mom seriously put him on a bus?"

"Yes."

My eyes bugged. "She put him on a bus alone, all confused about why he was in Shady Corners?"

Stuart said, "Lance volunteered to go with him. He's taking him home." The rabbit made a snuffling noise that must be a chuckle. "Seemed as though he was willing to do whatever he could to redeem himself for leading Xavier to your doorstep. Though his family has some small magical ability, what he saw downstairs was quite impressive and overwhelming for him."

"At least he tried to help. I saw him doing some spell work during the confrontation." I could forgive Lance for the mistake he'd made, working for Xavier. After all, the evil wizard wasn't exactly honest and forthcoming about his intentions. The only thing I could blame Lance for was being a bad judge of character.

That thought made me wonder what Xavier's aura looked like. A vision of oily, slinking, black slime crawling around the guy's perimeter crossed my mind. But it must not have been as obvious as that, or Lance would have been warned away when he saw it.

My stomach didn't care about Xavier's aura. "I'm hungry," I said unnecessarily, pretty sure the rumbling was loud enough for the rabbit's huge ears to pick up easily.

Stuart yawned and reached for me with a paw. I gave him a lift to the floor. "As am I. I'll meet you downstairs." He hopped away.

I made quick work of cleaning up and getting dressed—I had almost as many clothes at my bestie's house as mine—and went downstairs.

Isla rushed to me as soon as I put a toe into the kitchen. "How are you feeling?" She smashed me into a tight hug.

"Trouble breathing," I choked.

She pulled back, alarmed. "What? Is it your throat? Did he damage it?"

I shook my head. "No, you just hugged me too tight." With a wink, I stepped around her and headed for the coffee pot. "What's for breakfast? Smells great."

"Quiche."

"Mmm. My favorite." I rummaged in the cupboard for a to-go mug and pulled out one that said Caterers Like It Spicy.

"Not hanging out for long?" She gestured toward the mug.

I shook my head and poured a steaming cup. "I need to get to the office and check on the events schedule. See if there's anything Mira and Jed need help with. Also, I lost like half a day yesterday. I have to step on the gas with this murder investigation. But I'm not sure where to go with it next."

She pulled the quiche out of the oven and set it on a trivet. "What do you have so far?"

I sank into a kitchen chair and considered the question. "Roger changed the dye gun canister right before Candace shot it at Strom when he crossed the finish line. But Mom and I went and looked at the dye gun at the police station. The canister was empty, which means it only had one ball in it when it was shot at Strom." I paused, mulling it over.

"So, you think Roger is the bad guy?" She pulled out a long knife and sank it into the quiche.

"No. I mean, I don't know. But I believed him when he said he didn't do it." Did I? He hadn't answered immediately. And said he was glad Strom was dead.

Isla paused her cutting. "It may have been Candace. She could have switched the canister at the last minute before shooting at Strom."

"Huh. That's not a bad idea." I sipped coffee. "Oh, man. This is excellent."

Her expression brightened and she began cutting again. "I got whole beans and ground them this time. It's amazing how big of a difference that makes. It's a new blend, too. Got it at that herb place downtown."

"Downtown. That reminds me." I told her about Mom spotting Janelle heading into Axel's building the night before when we were on our way to Isla's to confront Xavier.

She served quiche onto two plates and came over, setting one in front of me and sitting across the table. "Why would she be visiting him?"

"I don't know." I worked on cutting my slice into bite-sized pieces. "Let's see. Linda said Janelle was having an affair with Strom, but Janelle denied it. Axel was Strom's best friend, and he's hanging around Linda an awful lot now. Mom and I wondered if the two of them were having an affair."

"Who, Axel and Janelle? I'd say that's a good bet."

I stopped with a bite of quiche halfway to my mouth. "What? I meant Linda and Axel."

Isla chewed and considered that. Then she shook her head. "Janelle and Axel were both there helping Linda after Strom died, remember? I think they were at the 5K together."

I lowered the untouched bite back to my plate and envisioned the scene again. "You're right. They were both there. Maybe she *was* visiting him last night." When we'd talked to Janelle, she'd insisted she wasn't having an affair with Strom because she was dating someone. Could it be Axel?

My thoughts raced like water over river rocks. A path formed in my mind. I jumped up.

"Ah-ah-ah." Isla pointed her fork at my plate. "Don't even think about leaving my amazing breakfast uneaten to go off chasing bad guys." She gestured downward with the fork. "Sit. Eat."

I dropped back onto the chair and shoveled two bites at once into my mouth. As soon as the quiche hit my tongue, I slowed down, savoring. "This is amazing."

"You've always loved my quiche." She grinned and cut another bite from her piece.

I couldn't argue with that. But while my mouth enjoyed the breakfast, my brain spiraled out toward what I needed to do next. Then I realized I'd monopolized the conversation so far. "Hey, how are you feeling about Lance? I heard he left with Xavier."

She didn't make eye contact and took a few minutes to respond. Then she set her fork down. "I'm okay. It isn't like we were serious or anything."

I studied her closely while she continued to avoid meeting my eyes. "You don't look exactly okay."

She puffed and slumped back in the chair. "I feel...confused. I mean, I kinda liked that jerk. I can't believe he duped me."

Ah. Now I understood. "You feel guilty you let him get close to me or something?"

She didn't answer.

"You couldn't have known. Besides, I think Lance is a decent guy who believed Xavier when he told him I stole his magic. In his mind, he was doing something good helping him find me." I reached over and squeezed her hand. "I think he's a decent guy. You could consider calling him when he gets home from his road trip."

A few emotions skipped across her face—confusion, disbelief, and then hope. "Maybe." Then she shook her head. "I don't need him. I'm busy enough with my business, and I'm sure another guy will come along."

"If you like him, you should call him. Don't miss out on a potentially cool experience because you're beating yourself up over something you couldn't have foreseen. The only person responsible for Xavier attacking me is Xavier. And he isn't going to remember it, so it's over."

Isla got up and grabbed the quiche off the counter, bringing it back and plopping it on the table. "It's possible you're right. But I'm going to have to give it some thought."

I nodded, but my mind was already on something else—the next steps I needed to take to solve Strom's murder.

ISLA DIDN'T LET ME out of the house until I'd had two pieces of quiche and topped off my coffee with hot stuff. She wasn't usually quite that motherly, and I assumed the behavior was related to my brush with death the night before. I wondered how long it would take for her to relax. Then I had a terrible thought. If *Isla* was feeling hover-y, my *real mom* was probably going to be unbearable.

Great.

Luckily, I'd had everything I needed at Isla's house to get myself ready for the day. I didn't need to go home and run into my mom yet. In fact, I had a different destination in mind when I hopped in the truck. I did wonder for a few minutes how the rest of them had gotten home the night before and knew I should text and make sure they were okay, but I pushed it from my mind. I'd do it when I was done with this next visit.

I put Stuart's tote on the front seat carefully. He popped his head out and nuzzled my hand.

Wow. Could our relationship be on the upswing? If it was, I was glad of it.

When I climbed into the driver's seat, I thought of Cam and pulled out my phone to text him. I found four texts from him from the evening before and that morning. I quickly sent one back, letting him know I was fine and that I'd try to meet up with him for lunch to explain more. I couldn't wait to tell him I'd faced Xavier, made it, and gotten rid of him. That monkey was off our backs now for good.

It was a relief, to be sure, but my mind was so caught up in the riddle of the murder mystery that I wasn't allowing myself the full basking experience. I promised myself to bask once Strom's killer was in custody.

I remembered I needed to stop by my office first, and I left Stuart napping in the tote with the windows cracked as I ran inside.

Mira looked up from her computer, then jumped to her feet. "How's it going? Did you figure out who killed Strom?" She rubbed her arms, though it was anything but cold in the building.

"I'm sorry. Not yet. But I think I'm getting closer. I'm actually on my way to hopefully find out some more information now."

The wrinkles etched between her brows didn't ease.

"Is everything going okay here? I'm sorry I've been MIA."

She shook her head. "It's fine. I'd rather you be working on getting Candace and Roger off the hook than hanging around here. I can handle work stuff."

So, she did know Roger was a suspect. "I'll get it figured out."

She forced a smile. "I know. Go ahead—get to it."

I turned to leave but then spun around and pulled her into a tight hug. "Things are going to be looking up soon. I promise." It was probably a bad idea to promise something like that, but there it was. In for a penny...as they say. I was determined to get Mira's smile back.

I hurried back to the truck with a renewed determination.

When I got to the animal shelter, Candace's car sat in the lot. I went through the front door and heard a cacophony of yips, trills, and barks coming from the dog kennels. I rang the bell on the counter, then glanced at the stack of mail still there.

"Oh, hi, Rory." Candace appeared in the lobby's doorway. "Everything okay with your rabbit?"

"Oh. Yeah. Actually, he's right here." I set the tote down, and Stuart hopped out.

Candace made a surprised noise. "Wow. You're carrying him around in your purse, huh? That's...different. I've seen people do it with small dogs but not bunnies."

"Yeah, I'm a trendsetter. Listen, I haven't gotten anywhere to speak of in the investigation, and I stopped by to see if you've thought of anything you could tell me that may help. But while I was waiting for you to come up, I happened to see this." I held up the mail from Janelle. "She was working with Strom—as his realtor." I twisted the envelope to catch the sunlight streaming in the front windows. "It looks like there's a check in here. What is Janelle paying you for?"

Candace's eyes darted from the envelope in my hand to the door and back. Then she looked at her feet. What was she feeling anxious about?

She cleared her throat and shifted her weight. "It's nothing. Give it to me." She held out her hand.

I crossed to hand it to her. "You know, if I'm going to clear your name with Sheriff Norton, you need to tell me everything you can possibly think of that could help. And that includes what relationship you have with Strom's realtor." I was trying for a gentle but firm tone, but it came out only firm.

Candace stiffened. She stuck the envelope in her jeans' back pocket and stared at me. I stared back. Finally, she looked away. "It's for some work I did for her, that's all. Nothing to do with Mr. Pearson's death, and I signed a non-disclosure agreement."

I frowned slightly. "I'll try not to divulge what you tell me unless I have to, but if I were you, I'd rather face a lawsuit over leaking information than a trial for murder." I kept my eyes on her face. "What work was Janelle paying you for?"

She skirted around me and started going through the rest of the stack of mail. "She came in here a few weeks ago. She looked around and saw some of the stuff that needs to be done around here." She turned away from the junk mail and finally looked at me. "Said she may be able to help me with some funds if I wanted to do something for her. I needed the money, so I agreed."

"What did you do?" I felt like I was on repeat. Why was Candace being so cagey?

"She wanted me to keep an eye on Linda Pearson."

I did not see that coming. "Keep an eye on her? Like how?"

"You know, follow her around. Report on where she went and who she was with. That's all. I did it for a week or so."

"Why did Janelle ask you and not a private investigator?"

"I'm probably cheaper. Mr. Pearson was footing the bill, after all. She said he directed her to come talk to me about the opportunity to make some money because he knew there was stuff I wanted done around here." Her mouth twisted. "Not *needed* done but *wanted* done. What a jerk. I almost said no on principle, but it seemed like easy money, and I did need it, so I agreed."

"What did you find out about Mrs. Pearson?"

"Nothing interesting happened the whole time I watched her. She went to ladies' meetings, shopped, hit the salon twice in one week. I jotted everything down and delivered the list to Janelle." She patted her pocket. "This is the payment. Hopefully, it'll keep this place going for another couple months after I repay my bail money."

I remembered her looking sad when she went through the mail the day before. She'd probably been upset the check hadn't arrived yet.

I peered closer at her face. It was lined and sagging with exhausted. "Are you doing okay?"

"I guess. I'm not sleeping great. Fear of being arrested for murder'll do that to you. I don't have anyone to take care of the animals if that happens. I mean, I know Mira will do what she can, but I can't expect her to give up her own job and life to do everything I usually do. The animals will have to be moved to other shelters." She sagged against the counter. "I don't know what I'm going to do."

"I understand. And I'm still working on it." I gentled my tone. "But you have to tell me everything. Even stuff you may not think is important like about Janelle asking you to spy on Mrs. Pearson."

Her eyes snapped upward to focus on my face. "You think that has to do with Strom's murder?"

"I don't know. It could. It's information, anyway, and I can use all of that I can get. So, if there's anything else you think of—anything at all, no matter how tiny, please call me, okay?"

"Okay."

I headed for the door.

"Rory?"

I paused and turned to look at her. "Yeah?"

"Don't forget Stuart."

I *had* forgotten him. My gaze swept the room, and I spotted my bunny sleeping next to a potted plant. I swept him up and put him back in his tote. He only opened one eye a slit and closed it again. Stuart must be exhausted from the events of the previous evening. I gently lifted the tote, thinking about how I no longer felt irritated about having to drag him around everywhere with me. Actually, it was kind of nice to have the company.

I decided to stop and get him the soft-sided carrier he wanted sometime that day, no matter what. He deserved it. Without him, I may not have been able to figure out how to defeat Xavier.

On my way back to the truck, I used one thumb to text my mom: *Is Sasha OK?*

She texted back almost immediately: *She's fine. Had pâté for breakfast and went back to bed.*

Thank goodness. Are the rest of you OK too?

Fine. So glad it's over. R U coming home?

I chuckled at her text abbreviation as I hoisted Stuart onto the passenger seat, shut the door, and leaned on it. *Soon. Need to see Linda.*

Come get me.

I typed in *No* but backspaced and hesitated. I remembered how having Mom there had kept Linda in check some at the farmer's market. Maybe I did need a wingman for this conversation. I typed *Be there in 10* and hurried around to the driver's side.

As I drove home, I thought about how nice it was to have so many people—and animals—behind me. I'd tried to get them all to safety while I confronted Xavier, but the truth was that, if they hadn't ignored me and showed up anyway, it was highly likely I would have failed. Goosebumps popped up on my arms at that thought.

I needed to stop pushing everyone away in the name of their own safety and embrace the fact that they wanted to help me. They were all adults who knew what they were getting into, after all.

And I needed them. I was better with their help.

I glanced at Stuart, still snoozing in the tote, and grinned. My life may not be conventional, but it wasn't boring. And I was well-loved.

Mom waited for me in front of the house, and she jumped in the truck when I pulled up. Immediately, I could tell a difference in her. Her vibe was lighter, happier. More like I remembered her before she left Shady Corners. She delivered a brilliant smile and then slipped on her Jackie-O sunglasses. "Okay. Let's go put this mystery to bed so we can properly celebrate Xavier being out of our lives for good." She pulled on her seatbelt.

I reached across Stuart's tote to grab her hand. "Thanks, Mom. You were so brave last night."

"Me?" She squeezed back. "Honey, you were amazing. As long as I live, I'll never forgive myself for bringing Xavier into our lives, but I'm so proud of you."

I shook my head. "If there hadn't been an Xavier, I may have never learned what I am or come into my full power. I only wish you hadn't had to leave for so long."

"I shouldn't have gone." Her voice was thick with emotion. "I should have told you years ago you were a spirit witch. Let you help figure out what to do about Xavier then." She twisted to face me squarely. "I should have trusted you."

I let go of her hand and started the truck. "It's over now. We made it through. And you're right—once we figure out who killed Strom, we can have a proper celebration. Now, let's go see what Linda knows about Janelle paying people to watch her."

Chapter 17

A locked gate stood at the end of the Pearsons' long driveway. I pulled up and stared blankly at it, then turned to my mom. "Fancy. How are we going to get in?"

"Let me try." She hopped out and advanced to a box mounted on one of the wrought iron posts. She pressed the button. I rolled down my window to listen. "Linda, it's Elaina Aspen. Can I come up and talk to you for a few minutes?"

There was a pause, and then Mrs. Pearson's tinny voice came through the box. "Elaina. Is this absolutely necessary? I'm quite busy this morning."

Mom glanced at me, then pushed the button again. "I'm afraid so. Sorry. We'll be as quick as possible."

There was another pause, and I thought she may refuse to let us enter, but the fear of looking bad to the church ladies held, and Linda said, "Step back please." Once my mom had danced away from the gate, it creaked open enough for me to get the truck through.

The driveway was at least a mile long, but finally, the house appeared before us, as huge and obnoxious as I'd expected it to be, complete with a tinkling fountain shaped like a mermaid out front. I rolled my eyes, threw the truck in park, and leaped out. Mom grabbed Stuart and met me at the front of the vehicle. My old, rusty red truck was as out of place in front of this mansion as a giraffe in the desert.

The front door opened before we got to it, and a man dressed in a beige suit led us in without a word. We crossed a marble foyer into a well-appointed den, where Linda sat sipping a mimosa. She gestured toward two more on a silver tray, and we each grabbed one and sat across from her, on the most uncomfortable, stiff couch ever. It was beautiful, though, cream with tiny lavender flowers, and I noticed Mom giving it an appreciative look. Me, I was more about function than form, and this thing was like sitting on a piece of plywood.

But the mimosa was delicious.

"What do you need?" Linda asked without small talk.

Fine with me. The less time in this uncomfortable house, the better. "Mrs. Pearson, I'm sorry to bother you during this difficult time, but we've learned that your husband's realtor paid someone to have you followed. Did you know about that, or do you have any idea why she may have done so?"

She set her drink on the delicate end table beside her and laced her fingers. "I suppose she and my husband were probably looking for some dirt on me, so he could file for divorce and not have to give me half of everything he has."

"So, you didn't have a pre-nup?" Mom ran her fingers over the rough upholstery, still enamored by the pretty pattern.

Linda barked out a laugh. "When we got married, Strom wasn't worth anything. We were deeply in love." Nostalgia crossed her face, and her lips turned downward. "It was only after he saw some success with rental properties that the money started coming in. We had no need for a pre-nuptial when we got married. We never had a clue we'd have so much." She looked around at all the expensive things in the room, and I got the feeling she was seeing something other than what was there. "We thought we'd live a moderate life. Have children. Be a normal couple."

The wistfulness in her voice was apparent, and Mom gave up studying the couch to focus on her. "Life had other plans."

Linda sniffed. "That's how things go. So, no, if Strom divorced me, he'd be giving up half of everything, at least, and that's why he was having an affair rather than leaving me. As I said, I assume he and his mistress were trying to prove I was doing something untoward, so he could divorce me without having to give up the house or pay alimony."

It made sense. "But wouldn't he have had to have some reason to believe you were doing something wrong to think of that?"

Her gaze snapped to mine. "I told you I wasn't having an affair." She grabbed her glass again and swirled the contents. "I wanted to, but I knew I couldn't, or I'd risk being put out of the marriage with nothing. So, I was biding my time. To catch him in the act or force him to give up and divorce me, so I could have the relationship I want." She finally smiled a little. "I'm a patient woman."

"Janelle denied having an affair with your husband," Mom said. "Do you have any proof?"

She pursed her lips. "Only the proof of a wife who knows her husband."

Mom and I exchanged a glance. That wasn't good enough for a murder investigation.

The doorbell rang, and Linda looked over her shoulder. Soon, the man in the beige suit appeared in the doorway with

Axel, who looked surprised to see us. "Sorry for interrupting. I came by to see how you're feeling today, Linda."

"Seamus, please bring Axel whatever he wants to drink," Linda said.

"Orange juice," Axel told beige-suit guy before striding forward. He put a hand on Linda's shoulder, and she touched it briefly with hers. But he addressed us. "Is there something I can help you with? Linda's been tired." The reproach was clear in his tone.

I shook my head and stood, putting the half-full mimosa glass on the tray. "We were just finishing up."

He gestured to the couch behind me. "Don't rush on my account. Sit and finish your drink. Thanks, Seamus." He accepted the orange juice with a smile.

I reluctantly sank back onto the world's most uncomfortable couch.

"Elaina and her daughter were asking me about Strom's affair with Janelle," Linda said before draining her mimosa and handing the empty glass to Seamus. She held up one finger, and the beige-suited server hurried off.

Axel perched on the edge of Linda's chair. "Oh, yeah? What do you want to know about it?"

"So, you also believe Strom was having an affair?"

He shrugged with only one shoulder. "He was with her a lot. I mean, he didn't tell me he was having an affair or anything, but I got the feeling there was more going on than business."

"You don't think he would have confessed to you, his best friend?" Mom put in.

He drank half the orange juice in one slug, drawing a slight frown from Linda. "Hard to tell. We were good friends, but there's some stuff even bros don't tell each other, you know?" He glanced at her. "And Strom knew what it meant for him if he was caught cheating."

So, Axel knew there was no pre-nup, and Linda may get awarded more during a divorce if Strom was proven to be cheating.

Mom leaned forward. "Is everything all set for the memorial service? Do you need help with anything?"

Linda shook her head. "Not unless you can create more time for me to get ready."

Axel jumped up and offered his hand to help Linda up as Robert returned with a refilled mimosa glass for her.

Mom and I rose with them. "Thanks for taking the time to answer our questions." I moved toward the door.

"I'm heading out too, but text if you need anything," Axel told Linda. He chugged the rest of the orange juice, handed the empty glass to Seamus, and followed us through the foyer and out the door. Once it was firmly shut behind us, he said, "I don't necessarily think Strom was cheating, you know. But believing he was makes his death easier for poor Linda to bear."

I narrowed my eyes. "I understand you wanting to make it easier for her, but Strom was murdered. It's important the facts come out, so his killer can be tracked down."

"It was the animal woman, right?" He headed down the steps. "I have to run, but thanks again for handling that produce list. Frees me up to do a little target practice today before the service." He grinned at us. "I'm hoping to surpass my record today."

His fancy BMW, though it was an older model, fit in better in front of the mansion than my truck, and I watched as he got in and pulled away. Something niggled at my brain about the conversation, but I couldn't put my finger on it.

"What now?" Mom asked, pulling open the truck door. She leaned in to check on Stuart. "Still sleeping."

I climbed in the driver's side. "There has to be some way to find out for sure whether Janelle was having an affair with Strom." I pulled away from the curb, steering around the fountain and back onto the long driveway. "But I can't figure out how."

"Asking her again isn't going to work," Mom said. "She's going to repeat what she said before—that she wasn't."

She was right. So, how could we find out for sure? "I may have an idea!"

Mom chuckled. "I'm getting used to hearing that. You know, you're very good at this, Rory. If you weren't such a fantastic event planner, I would say you should have gone into criminal justice."

I winced. "Yuck. I may be nosy, but I'm definitely not full-time investigator material. I've only solved the mysteries I have because they involved people important to me. I much prefer picking out linens and matching colors. Giving parties a little enhanced vibe with my holiday magic." I glanced at her. "But thanks."

"What's your idea, dear?"

We'd finally made it to the end of the long driveway. "We need to go to Janelle's office again." I turned the truck in that direction.

"But, like you said, she isn't going to fess up now if she didn't before."

"I know. We aren't going to talk to Janelle."

"We're not?"

"Nope."

She gave me a quizzical look but didn't ask more. We rode in silence to the realtor's office building.

We went in, and someone was behind the desk this time, a woman with a beehive hairdo. "Hi, there! Do you have an appointment with one of our realtors?"

"No, but we were hoping to see Troy."

From the corner of my eye, I watched Mom work to hide her surprise. I should have told her the plan before we came in.

The receptionist consulted her computer. "He's here and shouldn't be in another appointment right now." She came around the desk. "Let's see if he's available for you."

We followed her down the hallway. I glanced toward Janelle's office as we walked past, but the door was closed, and it was dark inside. *Good.* My gamble had worked. I'd been hoping she'd be out.

Troy was surprised but welcomed us into his messy office and dismissed the receptionist. "I remember you two. You're Janelle's clients." He picked up a stack of papers from a chair, then brushed crumbs off another, so we could sit.

"We were her clients, but she seems too busy for the level of service we need," I said. "In fact, she must be busy right now because she isn't here."

"Oh, yes, I could see that. She's been extremely busy since she started looking for development properties for Strom Pearson, like I said last time I saw you. I thought that would slow down with him being gone, but I guess she's caught up in a case of new love also. I believe she's with him now—she took the morning off and asked me to handle anything that came in for her."

That was our good fortune.

"New love?" Mom said with a casual tone. "You mean Janelle's recently started dating someone?"

"Yes, they've been together non-stop. She even brought him to our company bowling night this month. He wasn't very good." Troy's chest puffed up. "Got thirty points less than me. He didn't like it, either. Challenged me to a skeet shooting day, so now I have to figure out how to avoid that."

Mom chuckled. "Not a shooter?"

Troy shook his head. "No. But I get the idea Axel is. He told me he has an array of guns and ammunition. Offered to show me." He shuddered. "I don't like guns."

Mom and I exchanged a glance. What were the odds Janelle's boyfriend wasn't Axel Price, Strom Pearson's best friend? I didn't figure they were very high. He must be the boyfriend Janelle kept insisting she had.

"Was Janelle dating Axel when she was working with Mr. Pearson?" I asked, hoping to keep Troy answering our questions. I couldn't believe he hadn't gotten suspicious yet.

"Oh, yes." He sank into his chair, right on top of a couple thin folders stacked there. He crossed an ankle over the other knee and settled in, though I knew it couldn't be comfortable. Hopefully, whatever was in those folders wasn't too important. "I thought they may break up a few days ago when I heard them fighting in Janelle's office."

"Oh, that's too bad." Mom tsked and shook her head. "I hate to hear about young people in love having difficulties. I wonder what the problem was. Janelle seems so sweet and love-ly."

"She is, she is. A little snippy sometimes." He waved that off with a hand. "But yes, they were arguing quite vehemently. Axel was saying Janelle was getting pushed out of something, and he thought something needed to be done about it. She told him to calm down and let her handle it. That she was on top of things and knew exactly what to do. He told her she'd better handle it, or they'd both lose a million dollars. Then he stormed out." Troy's spine stiffened, and his eyes shifted to the doorway. "I've said too much. Please forgive me for gossiping and forget that, okay? How about you tell me what kind of house you're look-ing for, and we can get down to business?"

"Oh. Um. Sure. I need something with a nice big yard for my dog. And at least three bedrooms because I'm tired of shar-ing my bed. Within the town's limits because I don't want to be far from my office."

Mom's eyebrows rose into her frosted hair, and she shot me a wide-eyed look.

I looked away, not wanting to meet her eyes. "I've been thinking about getting a small place. If I can find one in the right price range." I remembered Mom's wistful expression when she heard about Linda and Strom's plan trip to Greece. My parents deserved some time alone together.

"Did you say sharing your bed?" Troy asked. Then he leaned forward and tapped a key, so his monitor woke up. "Never mind. None of my business. Let's see what's out there. How many bathrooms?"

"One is fine."

Mom interrupted, "Rory, if you don't want to share your bed with Sasha and Stuart, all you have to do is say so. And be firm about it. I'm sure they'll honor your wishes."

Troy's eyes almost bugged out.

I held up a hand. "It's not what you think."

He mirrored my motion with his own hand. "No need to explain. It's not my job to judge. It's my job to find your dream home." He clicked some keys, bringing up a list of houses.

"Can you print those off for me? I'll look at them and get back with you if I want to see any of them."

"Sure thing." He hit some buttons, and a printer behind him roared to life. He looked relieved to hear I'd be leaving soon. "You know, maybe you should go back to working with Janelle. If she started helping you, it's not ethical for me to take over."

"Yeah, yeah," I said. "No problem. I should have thought of that." I stood and accepted the stack of paper he handed me from the printer. "Sorry to take up your time."

"Oh, I wasn't doing anything anyway. But, yes, call Janelle if you want to see any of those houses. Bye, now." He looked decidedly nervous, and whether it was about my bedmates or his slip in telling us too much about his coworker, I didn't know. But I was glad for the invitation to leave and pulled my mother by the hand along with me up the hallway. I was glad Janelle's office was still dark and closed.

When we got outside, I turned to Mom. "Are you thinking the same thing I am?"

"I'm thinking it's a shame I had to learn that my daughter wants to move out in such a non-personal way. Is that what you're thinking?"

I groaned. "Mom. I'm not moving tomorrow or anything. I want to start keeping an eye out for a good deal. Can you focus please?"

She pressed her lips together and gave me a mom look. But then she said, "Sounds suspiciously like Janelle may have *handled* something, like she promised Axel she'd do during their fight."

"Something like Mr. Pearson?"

"Yep."

"Okay. But we have to figure out how to prove it. How are we going to do that?"

She wrinkled her nose for a moment. Then her forehead smoothed, and she smiled. "I may have an idea."

Chapter 18

I'd lived in Shady Corners my whole life and never been to the skeet range, which was on the same property as the gun range where people practiced shooting with rifles and pistols. No one I knew was into shooting, but I knew that it was a pretty popular pastime for others. When I was in high school, some of the kids were into it, and there was even an extracurricular team based on it.

When we pulled up to the range, nerves wrangled through my gut. "I'm not sure I want to be here. Isn't it dangerous?"

Mom wrinkled her nose. "Loud too."

As if to punctuate our conversation, shots rang out. Past the building in front of us was a large field where the skeet shooting was going on. Clay pigeons flew into the air and then erupted into a million pieces as folks used shotguns for target practice.

"We should just go in the building, honey, not out on the range. We can find some way to keep ourselves occupied until we spot Janelle with Axel. Or if they're not together, we'll get her to admit she's dating him. We may be able to get something more concrete out of her about what she meant when she told him she'd handle the problem of Strom Pearson."

It wasn't a bad idea. I could think of worse. I'd done worse. But Janelle seemed like a fairly sharp cookie to me. I wondered how likely it was that we'd get anything about of her.

Still, she had seemed worked up when we questioned her before. We could try pushing on that anxiety to get her to spill.

"Okay, let's give it a try."

Bring me with you! Stuart stuck his furry head out of the tote.

You're awake!

I've been awake. His tone was affronted. *I was only resting my eyes.*

I chuckled and grabbed the tote handles, pulling them across the seat and onto my shoulder. I followed Mom across the parking lot and through the front door. The inside reminded me of a golf course's clubhouse. On one side was a sport shop that sold various things associated with guns and shooting. On the other was a small restaurant. Signs indicated the indoor shooting range was down a long hallway past the restaurant, and I could hear muffled sounds that confirmed it. The far wall of the room was floor-to-ceiling windows looking out on the skeet range.

Near the front door was an Easter display. A huge basket, easily four feet across, stood on a table barely big enough for it. A mound of colorful jellybeans peeked over the top. In front of the basket stood a wicker chair with a sign perched on it proclaiming that the Easter bunny would be visiting for pictures with kids at one o'clock.

"There's Axel," Mom whispered, and I spotted him out there too. He was with a group of five or six other men.

Janelle wasn't with him. "Where do you think she is?"

Mom's gaze moved toward the restaurant. "If I were her, I'd be in there."

"Let's get some lunch, then." I headed across the room.

The restaurant was casual dining, seat yourself, and fairly busy. It took me a minute to spot Janelle at a small table by the window. She had a glass of iced tea and an open laptop in front of her.

I headed for a nearby table, but Mom veered off and went straight for Janelle's. I squeaked out her name, but she ignored me and continued, so I had no choice but to follow or be left standing awkwardly with a rabbit in a tote on my shoulder.

Janelle looked up when Mom got to her. She took off her reading glasses. "Can I help you?" She shut the laptop cover.

Mom took a seat without being offered one, and I scooted onto the chair next to her. Janelle's expression morphed rapidly from bewildered to irritated. "I'm pretty busy—this is a working lunch." She gestured to the computer.

"Perfect," Mom trilled. "Because we don't have much time. We're working too." She glanced out the window at the men shooting. "We have it on good authority that the boyfriend you told us about before is Axel Price."

She followed Mom's gaze and then jerked her eyes back to us. "So?"

"So, you were heard having a pretty substantial argument with Axel that had to do with your work for Strom Pearson. You said something incriminating during that argument, and we want to know what you meant by it."

I considered jumping in to help but snapped my mouth shut. My mother was doing a fine job all on her own. Maybe she was the one who should consider a second career in crime investigation. I should definitely share whatever pittance I got from the police department for this job with her.

Janelle's eyes narrowed to slits. "You went to my office and talked to my co-workers to get dirt on me?"

I shook my head. "Not dirt. Information. We're investigating a murder—it's nothing personal."

She shifted her glare to me. "You're not even a cop."

"Nope. But I'm hip-deep in this investigation." I jerked my chin. "And so is she. So, either you tell us what we need to know, or we make ourselves a heck of a lot more annoying than we already have been."

It was partly a bluff. It wasn't like I could make a big scene in public or anything. Casey had told me not to do that, and I didn't want to find out what happened if I defied her orders so blatantly. But Janelle didn't know that, and I was betting she didn't want anyone in the skeet club to hear us questioning her about a murder. Gossip traveled fast in Shady Corners, and she made her living as a realtor on word of mouth. Controversy was her enemy.

Her lips hardened into one grim line, and if she could have done it by sheer dirty look, I felt strongly I'd be dead or severely maimed. "Fine," she ground out. Then she puffed out some air and deflated. "Axel is a sweetie. When we started dating, I wasn't doing all that great selling houses. I'd sell one every six months or so, and I wasn't making much after the fees I need to pay the broker. So, he came up with a way to help me."

I shifted the tote on my lap so Stuart would be more comfortable. I was getting used to holding him. He didn't feel as heavy and awkward as before. "What was his idea?"

"His best friend—Strom—wanted to branch out into development properties. Axel said he could get me a deal with him. He set up a meeting, and he helped me through it, basically acting as a go-between, helping me figure out how to woo Strom and continually putting in good words for me. We ended up making a deal that I'd help him find properties, and he'd pay me my commission plus an extra cut on top of that."

Mom's eyelashes fluttered as her eyes widened. "That doesn't sound like it's on the up-and-up. Why would Strom agree to that for run-of-the-mill realtor services?" She leaned closer. "Were you doing something illegal to get him the deals?"

Janelle's neck swiveled as she looked around to see if anyone was near enough to hear. Then she leaned forward, too, and I was the third to get closer to hear her soft tone. "I ignored other offers. Put other buyers off however I could. Didn't put in their offers but said I did. I arranged it so Strom would get the deals at ten percent, at least, under asking price. It took a lot of finagling and staying on my toes to elbow other realtors out. But I was doing it and well too." She lifted her chin. "So, it wasn't fair when Strom told Axel he was cutting me out of my extra money."

"And Axel was outraged on your behalf," Mom offered.

Janelle nodded. "He was downright angry. I told him I'd handle it, though. And I tried. I asked Candace to spy on Mrs. Pearson. If she was able to get proof that she was cheating on him like I thought she was, I could present it to Strom, and he'd be so happy about the chance to divorce her without losing everything that he'd be happy to reinstate our original deal."

"So, it wasn't Strom who asked you to hire Candace," I said.

She shook her head. "Axel knew Candace had money problems because he'd been to the shelter with Strom."

"There's something I don't understand," Mom said. "Why did you believe Linda was cheating in the first place?"

"Axel suspected it because of some strange behavior he noticed when he was at their house hanging out with Strom. Linda came in late at night several times," Janelle said. "Plus, Strom was pretty open with Axel that his marriage wasn't great." Her phone buzzed, and she glanced at it. "I have to take this. Need to make a living without Strom now." She turned in her seat, dismissing us, and answered the phone.

Mom frowned, and I could almost see her mother wheels turning. She wasn't happy Janelle was getting away with cheating. Once I was on my feet with Stuart balanced on my shoulder, I tugged her up too. "Let's go."

I could tell she wanted to stay and lecture Janelle, but she let me lead her away. When we were far enough, I said, "We can always put in an anonymous tip to her broker when this is over if we want to. Hopefully she's learned her lesson on cheating, though."

"So, you don't think she killed Strom?"

Finding myself suddenly distracted, I didn't answer. Instead, I headed for the sport shop. Over my shoulder, I said, "I'm not sure, but I have a feeling I know how to find out."

Chapter 19

This is ridiculous.

Shh!

I'm not even talking out loud. Why on Earth would I need to be quiet? To punctuate his point, Stuart pitched sideways in his tote, so I had to lunge to regain our center of gravity. *I'm simply trying to tell you it's unbelievably silly for us to be hiding behind a giant Easter basket.*

I set the tote beside me, reached over my head into the basket, and retrieved a handful of jellybeans. I dropped them in with Stuart. *Is this enough to silence your protests? And insults?*

Protests, yes. Insults, no. But Stuart munched away, and blessedly, I only had to listen to his little groans of happiness instead of the sharp-tongued complaints for a moment.

I peeked around the edge of the basket. It was almost one o'clock, and the Easter bunny had arrived, wearing a full-blown suit complete with a pull-over head. He shuffled toward the chair in front of the basket, slumping as though it was the last thing he wanted to do.

Janelle came out of the restaurant. She'd been in there so long I'd started to think she was planning on pulling an all-dayer. Cuz that was totally a thing. But now, she paced in front of the windows, keeping an eye on the skeet players on the lawn. Before long, Axel's group headed for the building, laughing and banging each other on the backs like ball players.

Skeet shooting seemed like a macho pursuit. At least for this group of men.

Janelle bit her lip, arms crossed, and hovered near the door. When Axel came through, she snagged the arm of his shirt and yanked him away from the others, drawing a frown from him. She kept pulling until he was ten feet from the group of men, thankfully, closer to where I crouched behind the basket, silently cursing my hamstrings for cramping up and making my eyes water.

"Rory Aspen and her mother ambushed me in the restaurant," Janelle hissed.

Axel's eyes flashed, but his tone was indifferent. "So? I told you—there's nothing to worry about."

"That's easy for you to say. They acted like they think I killed Strom. And if that gets out..."

He grabbed her arms and hunched to look straight in her eyes. "It's not going to get out. I told you to let me handle this."

"I know that's what you said, but you didn't say I was going to have to deal with nosy event planners and their super annoying mothers."

I scowled. Whose mom was she calling annoying? Cuz *my* mom was a superstar. I had half a mind to stand up and tell Janelle off—if my hamstrings wanted to cooperate, which they didn't. I winced again and jabbed a fist into the most painful one, incrementally adjusting my weight, trying to relieve the pain.

"Kill 'em with kindness," Axel suggested in a low tone. "Be extra nice—sickly sweet if you have to. Get them off your track however you can. It's that simple."

She glanced around, eyebrows drawn down. "It seemed simple at first, but it's getting harder. When is it going to end?"

"When they arrest the animal woman," he assured, giving her arms a rub before dropping his hands. "Or the caterer dude. Soon."

"Are you sure they're going to do that?" She rubbed her own arms where Axel had done it a moment before.

"Yep." He winked. "Don't worry. The heat'll be off you soon."

A scuffle on the other side of the basket drew my attention. Several kids hung off the Easter bunny's arms, squealing with delight. He gave two quick jerks and sent them flying. One bumped into the basket, bumping me onto my behind. "Erg."

"I want the whole thing to be over," Janelle said. "Like, all of it. I think I want out."

Axel shook his head sharply. "I'm almost in with Linda. She likes me, I can tell. I think after the funeral, she'll feel better about taking on a boyfriend." His lips twisted in a sneer. "She's very proper and doesn't want to be considered gauche for taking on a man before her husband's buried. Once we're together, I'll be able to siphon enough money out of her estate to keep both of us on easy street."

Janelle's eyes darted to the bunny, who stood with his hands on his hips. It was hard to tell because of the perpetually smiling head, but I could swear the person inside the suit was scowling at the kiddos.

"I hope easy street is worth it," Janelle muttered.

Axel started to turn away.

"They're leaving. That's my cue," I whispered to Stuart. His only answer was smacking lips and groans of sugar-induced happiness.

I pushed painfully to my feet and limped out from behind the basket, stepping in front of Axel. "You know, if you ask me, easy street is overrated. Working hard for what you have in life is the way to go. And not murdering people goes a long way toward making sure you have a happy life too."

A couple of nearby parents heard me and shuffled their kids away, casting uneasy glances back at us. I kept my eyes on Axel's face.

"I'm starting to get irritated with you," he said. "You're very nosy."

I ignored that. "It took me a while to figure it out. I could claim distraction because I had some personal stuff going on that split my attention, but that would be whiney, so I won't do it. What I will say is this one was tricky to figure out. But I did. You changed the dye canister after Roger did. Before Candace shot it at Strom."

His eyes slid to Janelle and back to me. He didn't say anything.

I continued, "I remember you both being there, helping Linda after Strom was killed. You acted the role of best friend while simultaneously edging your way into Linda's consciousness. But the real reason you were there was to switch those canisters and make sure your best friend was gone. Because you weren't making headway in getting any of his money flowing your way while he was alive."

Dimly, I noticed my mom standing by the sport shop, watching us. But I kept staring at Axel.

"You can't prove that," he spat.

"You framed Candace. Or Roger. You didn't care who went to jail. You wanted to get rid of Strom because he cut Janelle out of the extra money she'd earned doing illegal real estate stuff for his development deals."

Janelle's face reddened, and she stepped back and looked at her feet. Probably thinking about how her career was over now that I'd let that bit of information out in public.

Because people were standing around watching us. Parents had gathered most of the kids close but stood around the edges of the room. The Easter Bunny seemed fully engrossed in the drama as well, still standing in front of the huge basket with only a few children left near him.

"For a while, I thought Janelle killed him," I said. "But she was only your puppet. You posed as her boyfriend to gain her trust and get her to do the illegal stuff for Strom, pretending you were helping her. But I have no doubt you would have figured out how to get most of that money away from her if she ever did get paid. And when it became clear she wasn't going to get the money, you thought of another plan."

Axel looked around, seeming to realize for the first time there were others in the room. He laughed. "She's a little out there, isn't she, folks? Armchair sleuth, I guess. Must watch too many crime shows."

"Oh, no, I hate crime shows." I wrinkled my nose. "Too violent and scary. What I do like is making sure criminals in Shady Corners get put behind bars. That's why I had a little talk with Gordon here." I nodded toward the silver-haired man next to

Mom in the doorway of the sport shop. "After a chat about how potentially dangerous you were, he told me all about the specially sized canisters of shrapnel you ordered to have made for you overseas. Ones that would fit the dye guns at my event. It was a believable story you gave him—that you wanted to show off for some of your buddies at a skeet party. But that isn't what you needed them for. They were to kill your best friend."

In a flash, Axel reached into his waistband and pulled out a pistol. He pointed it at my chest, which responded by tightening to the point of causing me to be almost unable to breathe.

I did not expect that. Pretty dumb of me not to, given where we were and how much Axel liked guns and ammunition.

Gasps went up in the crowd, and chaos erupted as everyone headed for the doors. The Easter Bunny grabbed the few remaining kids near him and shoved them behind his body.

"You think you're so smart. I didn't go through all this to have you snatch it from me. Strom didn't deserve the money he had. Neither does Linda. They aren't good people. Thanks to me, no one has to deal with Strom anymore. And now, no one will have to deal with you and your nosiness either."

I wanted to tell him how flawed his thinking was, since there were about a dozen witnesses here, and he wouldn't be able to kill me, walk out, and continue with his plan to squeeze money out of Linda. But he was clearly crazy, and reasoning wouldn't work.

I didn't take my eyes off the gun as Axel's trigger finger began to squeeze. I pulled on the web of energy around us—the strongest one because of the time of year and the event going on. The web of Easter spirit. The energy of new beginnings. Of change and expectation. I drew it in, gave it my intention, and pushed it out toward Axel's gun.

He squeezed the trigger.

Several things happened at once. Janelle shoved me violently, and I crashed into the giant Easter basket. Jellybeans erupted into the air like lava, spewing everywhere.

The side of Axel's head was pelted by the small colorful candies, and his gun hand went wildly off to the right as he shot.

The gun only clicked. Rage crossed his face, and Axel dropped the jammed pistol and lunged for me. His feet shot out in opposite directions as he skated over jellybeans. I scrabbled backward like a crab, slamming into the basket again. This time, it toppled over me, completely trapping me underneath as the remaining jellybeans rained on my head. Frantically, I tried to get it off, finally managing to raise the rim enough to see the action unfolding. Axel had regained his footing and came toward me, crunching more carefully over the jellybeans now.

I tried to figure out how to stop him without revealing I could do magic.

Then the Easter bunny leaped between Axel and me, holding up his own weapon. With the other hand, he pulled off his head. "Axel Price, you're under arrest for the murder of Strom Pearson. Put your hands up."

Axel's eyes nearly popped out, but he slowly raised his hands.

Casey Norton glanced over her shoulder at me, looking madder than a cat in a bathtub. "You're fired," she spat.

"What? Why? I figured out the murderer *and* got a public confession in front of the sheriff." I shoved the basket the rest of the way off and climbed up carefully. Stuart hopped over and sat on my foot.

"Do you have any idea how hot and stinky it is inside that rabbit suit?" Casey's mouth and nose twisted in disgust. As two officers hurried in and cuffed Axel, she holstered her weapon inside the bunny suit's waistband and turned to me. "Besides, this is a public place. When you called, you didn't give me time to tell you this was a stupid idea. You hung up on me. What if someone got hurt when he shot at you?" She looked furious.

I couldn't tell her I'd magically jammed the gun with fresh dirt and flowers. She'd have to wonder how they got in there when forensics found them. Instead, I advanced and threw an arm around her shoulders before she could react. "All's well that ends well." I held out a handful of jellybeans. "Want some?"

Chapter 20

"It's a beautiful night." Cam squeezed me closer into his side as we swayed slowly on the wooden porch swing he and Dad had wrestled into the back yard and watched the bonfire.

"It sure is. Very nice for May. I hope the warm weather is here to stay." I leaned my head on his shoulder. "Now that Axel's in jail and Xavier is gone, I feel like I can enjoy summer to the fullest."

I felt him grin, and he squeezed me tighter. "You can say that again. Though I want to hear more about what happened with Xavier. I still wish you'd called me to help you that night."

Twisting to peer up at him, I raised my eyebrows. "I know you want to protect me and all, but I'm the one with magical abilities. I think I'm best suited to fight off a wizard, don't you?" I gave his chin a playful kiss to take the sting out of the words.

"I guess so. But I don't have to like it." He winked at me.

"No, you don't. That's true." I lay my head back down and watched Piper bounce around the back yard. She couldn't decide who to visit. Mira and Roger worked at the picnic table, chopping, dicing, and mixing sides for dinner. Candace sat on the bench chatting with them. Dad and Jed threw a football back and forth. Mom and Isla worked at the grill together. "Look at that." I pointed to where Sasha and Stuart curled up together on the back porch, snoozing away. Likely, they couldn't resist a nap but didn't want to miss the dinner bell.

I thought about how happy Stuart had been when I presented him with the new soft-sided carrier I bought. He'd been just like a kid at Christmas. It had made me feel good.

"Adorable." Cam pulled back, adjusting himself to look into my eyes. "So, you're sure this is the end of Xavier's threat, right?"

I held up two fingers. "Scout's honor. He's gone for good. He has no magic and no memory of wanting to kill me."

Cam sagged in relief. "Thank goodness. Okay, I feel like we can relax and enjoy life now. Hey, do you like camping?"

"You know it." I leaned forward to kiss him, feeling happy and carefree for once.

"Aspen!" Casey Norton's sharp voice made me jump away from Cam, like we'd been caught making out. I had to remind myself we weren't teenagers.

"Yeah?" I stood and made my way over to meet her.

"Listen, I'm sorry I gave you a hard time at the skeet place. I wanted to let you know I appreciated the help on Strom's case." She swallowed hard and forced out the next words. "You did good."

"Thanks," I said brightly. "Oh, and I quit."

She blinked a few times. "You quit? What do you mean?"

"I don't want to solve mysteries anymore. If we have another murder in Shady Corners, you're on your own."

Her lips turned downward. "But you're so nosy. And bossy. You're great at solving mysteries. People confess just to get you to shut up."

"Hardy har-har." I crossed my arms. "I'm serious. I'm retired from being a detective. Hire someone else. Oh, but you do need to pay what you owe me." I glanced at Cam. "I'm going to use the money for a nice camping trip."

Casey looked like she wanted to argue, but she only shook her head. "Fine. I'll see you around." She started to leave.

"Hey! Why don't you stay for dinner?"

"Really?" She glanced around the yard. "I don't want to impose."

"You're not an imposition. You're a friend. Stay and hang out with us."

She hesitated, then nodded. "If you're sure."

"I am."

She wandered off, and Mom took her place. "It's a nice night."

"Sure is."

"Honey, I wanted to talk to you about what you said in Troy's office—that you're looking for a house. I want you to know you're welcome to stay with us for as long as you want."

"I know. But I want my own place. And I want you and Dad to have your space. It's time." I smiled at her. "You sacrificed a lot to keep me safe from Xavier. You had too much time away from Dad. The two of you lovebirds deserve some peace and quiet."

She tilted her head. "Okay, if you're sure. But you don't have to rush. We love having you here." With a last smile, she headed for the fire.

I waved at Cam and made my way to Isla. She turned hot-dogs on the grill. "Another adventure concluded, eh?"

"Yep," I said. "Did you decide what to do about Lance?"

She shook her head. "No, but he did call me last night. Said he left Xavier at home, doing fine. No indication he remembered anything. Lance is on his way back to Ann Arbor." She set down the tongs and turned to face me. "Did you know he thought you may have killed Strom?"

I thought back to how Lance had acted about me investigating. "Makes sense, I guess."

She tipped her head to watch fireflies zip by. "I think I'm ready to forget men and mysteries and magic for a few months and have a great summer like we used to. Hang out on the beach and get tan. Stay up late singing around a bonfire. Dance under the moon. Laugh like crazy and listen to music too loud. Eat too much and make a million memories. There's nothing like summer in Michigan." She held out her hand, fisted, with the pinky up. "You in, bestie?"

I smiled and grabbed her pinkie with mine. "I'm *so* in." I wrapped her in a hug and let myself enjoy the feeling of finally being free. Then I let her go and looked around at my family and friends. My sweet, supportive boyfriend. My dog and my familiars.

I felt like the luckiest witch in the world. It was a new beginning, and I was totally here for it.

About Paula Lester

Sign up for Paula's newsletter to receive information on book releases, other fun information, book recommendations, promos, and more: https://sendfox.com/lp/10q2rm
You can see all of Paula's books at: www.paulalester.com

———— ∞ ————

Works by Paula Lester:

———— ∞ ————

**Beachside Books Magical Cozy Mysteries
(Co-Authored with Lisa B. Thomas)**
Pasta, Pirates and Poison
Apples, Actors and Axes
Grits, Gamblers and Grudges
Candy, Carpenters and Candlesticks
Meatballs, Mistletoe and Murder
Honey, Hearts and Homicide

———— ∞ ————

**Crystal Springs Cozy Witch Mysteries
(Co-Authored with M.E. Harmon)**

Dead Witch Talking (prequel novella)
A Witch Too Late
A Witch Too Hot
A Witch Too Bright
A Witch Too Dead
A Witch Too Frozen
A Witch Too Soon

**Cruise Ship Cozy Mysteries
(Co-Authored with M.E. Harmon)**
Cruising for a Bruising
Angling for a Strangling
Yearning for a Burning

Sunnyside Retired Witches Community Mysteries
Ghostly Trails
A Bottle Full of Djinn
Loony Town
Mummy Issues
Clairvoyant Clues
Boss Blues
Engine Repairs
Wedding Whack

Sunnyside Magical Bakery Cozy Mysteries
Sugar Skulls and Suspects

Superior Bay Witch Doctor Mysteries
Witch Doggone Killer?
The Affairs of Witches
Witch Way Out? (Coming Soon)

Tessa Randolph Grim Reaper Cozy Mysteries
(Co-Authored with Christine Zane Thomas)
Grim and Bear It
The Scythe's Secrets
Reap What She Sows

Paranormal Posterity Series: Paranormal Women's Fiction
Cozy Mysteries
Plucked
Aurora Aspen Magical Holiday Mysteries
Claus for Concern
Crush and Burn
Run or Dye

www.ingramcontent.com/pod-product-compliance
Lightning Source LLC
Chambersburg PA
CBHW031042160726
47991CB00005B/2001